A ROGUE TO CHERISH

ROGUES OF THE LOWLANDS
BOOK THREE

BY
HILDIE MCQUEEN

ARE YOU SIGNED UP FOR DRAGONBLADE'S BLOG?

You'll get the latest news and information on exclusive giveaways, exclusive excerpts, coming releases, sales, free books, cover reveals and more.

Check out our complete list of authors, too!

No spam, no junk. That's a promise!

Sign Up Here

www.dragonbladepublishing.com

Dearest Reader;

Thank you for your support of a small press. At Dragonblade Publishing, we strive to bring you the highest quality Historical Romance from some of the best authors in the business. Without your support, there is no 'us', so we sincerely hope you adore these stories and find some new favorite authors along the way.

Happy Reading!

CEO, Dragonblade Publishing

Additional Dragonblade books by Author Hildie McQueen

Rogues of the Lowlands Series
A Rogue to Reform (Book 1)
A Rogue to Forget (Book 2)
A Rogue to Cherish (Book 3)

Clan Ross Series
A Heartless Laird (Book 1)
A Hardened Warrior (Book 2)
A Hellish Highlander (Book 3)
A Flawed Scotsman (Book 4)
A Fearless Rebel (Book 5)
A Fierce Archer (Book 6)
A Haunted Scot (Novella)
Highland Knight (Novella)
Stones of Ard Cairn (Novella)

The Lyon's Den Series
The Lyon's Laird

Pirates of Britannia Series
The Sea Lord
The Sea Lyon

De Wolfe Pack: The Series
The Duke's Fiery Bride

CHAPTER ONE

Glasgow, Scotland, April 1823

"D O YOU OR do you not have the money?" Miles Johnstone's whiskey-colored gaze pinned Grant Murray's.

His lordship swished the brandy in his glass, legs outstretched as if he had not one worry. However, his impatient huff told Grant differently. "The sooner you obtain the capital for our venture, the sooner I can get on with acquiring mine."

Around the room, the other two men, Evan Macleod, the owner of the home they were currently in, and Henry Campbell, a reformed gambler, looked on with interest.

All four had been friends for years; there was little they didn't know about each other. Unlike Miles, who was titled and quite wealthy, Grant and the other two men came from well-established, but untitled, families in Glasgow.

Just two short months earlier, they'd met in this exact room, where Evan had presented them with a proposition to make a fortune. All they had to do was come up with the capital to sponsor a ship that was headed for the West Indies. The ship would return with spices and other precious commodities that they could sell for ten times their investment. Each man's portion was quite sizable and therefore hard to attain, but they were determined to come up with it by whatever means possible.

The problem was that none of them, except for Miles, had much of an income and couldn't ask their families for help. Both Grant and Evan had become estranged from their fathers. In

Grant's case, he'd done something his father deemed unforgiva-
ble, and he'd been promptly cut off. As for Evan, at a young age,
he had demanded and subsequently squandered his entire
inheritance. And lastly, Henry had been reduced to a small
monthly stipend by his father for costing the family a fortune in
gambling debts.

Because of this, they'd needed to come up with ways to obtain the money needed to sponsor the ship, so they'd decided to
take advantage of their roguish reputations by seducing women,
or even marrying debutants with sizeable dowries. The four men
met each week to discuss the progress of the sponsorship for the
ship. If any of them could not come up with their portion, they'd
all have to scramble for the needed amount, so they'd given
themselves until the end of the current month to come up with it.

Being who they were, they'd even embarked in a wager, of
sorts. So far, Evan and Henry had come up with their portions,
neither by actually seducing someone with money, but by being
seduced by love. It had turned out well for Evan, whose wife
came with a large dowry, and for Henry, who'd reclaimed a huge
amount owed to him from a card game in which he'd wagered
his life.

Miles, not to be left out of the wager, had decided that he
would procure the capital without touching his own money. He'd
then challenged Grant to come up with his portion first, and once
that was accomplished, he promised, he'd acquire his within a
week.

Grant was determined to win the wager. "Lucinda has promised a deposit will be made into my account within days," he said,
his voice much surer than he felt. "Should be a day or two at
most."

"Bravo!" Henry exclaimed. "I am glad that we will all be able
to sponsor the ship and soon be richer for it." A grin split his
handsome face. "Then it will be up to you, Lord Johnstone, to
come up with your portion."

Miles once again looked at Grant. "I will believe it when you show proof of a deposit. Not a moment before."

"Here, here," Evan said, lifting his glass. "I, too, will only believe it then."

"You both wound me," Grant replied, giving them the most pained expression he could muster. "I have put days... no, *weeks* of effort into romancing Lucinda Roberts. She is enamored with the idea of a young lover and will do anything to keep me happy." He smiled, looking at Miles. "Soon, I am sure, she will grow bored with me and move on, but not before gifting me for time well spent."

"There was the incident, at Henry's family home, which may change things," Miles replied lazily. "Her son is quite put out about your... *entanglement* with his mother. Every gossip in town is having a field day over the incident at the engagement party."

Grant waved a hand in the air, dismissing the words. "Lucinda is very independent. I am sure her son will not influence anything she does."

After a moment, Miles shrugged. "We will see."

Just then, Norman, the butler, appeared in the arched doorway. "Dinner is served," he said.

Everyone stood and followed him across the foyer to the dining room, except Evan, who hung back. The tall man met Grant's gaze. "Felicity and I are going to spend a few days at the Campbell estate. Henry's mother is planning a picnic and that sort of thing."

Grant gave his friend a look that expressed his distaste for such a bland event. "How positively domestic."

At the comment, Evan laughed. "True, and I would rather do nothing more."

Grant frowned at Evan's retreating back. How strange it was to see two of his friends settled with wives and not seeming to mind it one bit.

Perhaps in the distant future, he too would feel so strongly for someone that he'd consider marriage. However, just the thought of losing his freedom at the current moment made him shudder.

After supper, he and Miles had gone to the Grant Hotel and spent several hours at a card game. The Grant Hotel's club was not quite of the same level as a place where the elite gentlemen gathered, but it was a place where men of means congregated. He often met with his friends there. An aged whiskey had been offered to them and liking the taste of it, he'd overindulged.

Now, the house was silent, which prompted him to linger in bed. The inside of his mouth was sour, his tongue heavy, and he eyed the rope pull, considering if he should summon for something to drink. It was large, and comfortable, the mostly gray-colored bedding plush. Just a trickle of sunlight managed to get through the center of the matching draperies, giving enough light to look around the room.

His gaze hesitated on a floral painting. The bold brush strokes in red, green, and blue did not make his room feminine but seemed to reinforce the masculine feel of the space. Even the books on the table near the window, along with a quill and ink, or the lone decanter with two glasses beside them, added touches that left no doubt who slept there.

He'd not taken much interest in the room, other than to place whatever gifts arrived for him atop a bookcase or sometimes on the bedtable. Usually, the trinkets were placed into the trunk at the foot of his bed.

Grant exhaled, straining to hear if anyone was up and about. It was probably almost nine, or perhaps half past. It didn't matter, there was little to do that day.

But then, there was a rap on the door and Grant croaked out a husky, "Come in."

"Tea, sir?" The butler, who seemed to know exactly what was needed, entered with a tray. "I've taken the liberty of asking Cook to make some toasted bread as well."

Grant could kiss the man. "Thank you, Norman. You are a

godsend."

The man's craggy face softened. "You are very welcome, sir."

When he'd finally risen and dressed, Grant decided the weather would be perfect for a ride into town. Perhaps he'd visit Miles or take a turn through the park where people would be out, enjoying the sunny day. As he pondered, the sound of horses drew him to the window where he spotted a carriage pulling up to the house. Since his sister Felicity and her husband Evan were both gone, it was strange that a visitor would come for them and, as he very rarely entertained, whoever came was definitely not there to see him.

The driver climbed down and went to the carriage door, opened it, and assisted a woman out into the sun-filled late morning. She was not familiar, which convinced him that she was not there to see him. But because the carriage was quite luxurious, it made her appearance of sturdy shoes and worn clothes curious.

It was then that he noted the seal on the door; it was the Roberts' crest. Lucinda Roberts, his lover, was a demanding older woman with a voracious, and at times shocking, sexual appetite. She was no doubt put out that he'd not spent time with her in the last couple of days. Grant realized she had sent the woman, probably with a message for him.

He watched as the maid scrambled up to the front door and knocked, her small hand barely making a sound against the thick wooden door. Norman, who apparently had excellent hearing, must have heard the soft knocks because moments later, he appeared at Grant's door. "Sir, a young woman is here to speak to you."

"Thank you, Norman. I will be down shortly," Grant drawled, not in the mood to be summoned by his demanding and much older lover, who took every opportunity to parade him in front of her peers. The action always garnered varying reactions. Some studied him as if he was some sort of artifact, others with glares of disapproval, or in the case of the more adventurous, resulted in invitations for a tryst.

Upon reaching the first floor, Grant didn't see the young woman. She wasn't in the drawing room either, so he went in search of Norman.

"Where is she?" he asked, annoyed.

"I left her in the drawing room, sir," the butler replied, hurrying to the room.

It was then Grant saw her. She stood near the far corner of the room, looking out the window.

"Right," Grant said and turned back to study the woman. She was of average height, with a slender figure and dark auburn hair that was pinned up under a simple kerchief. When he cleared his throat, she jumped and turned to look at him.

"I apologize, sir, I was admiring the gardens. They are beautiful," she said. He opened his mouth to respond, but she continued, "It is quite a lovely day, is it not? I do adore flowers, and these are quite well-tended. I can only imagine the garden would be the perfect place to sit and..." She trailed off as her almond-shaped blue eyes widened and her cheeks turned bright red. She covered her mouth with both hands. "I am so sorry for going on, sir."

Grant couldn't help but chuckle. He looked to the window. "My sister spends a great deal of time out there. She is quite proud of her garden and will be glad when I tell her someone admired it so."

"Thank you, sir," the young woman said. "For you." She held out a paper. "From Lady Roberts."

Of course. Grant let out a sigh and for some reason felt uncomfortable by the young woman's looking on while he read the message. "Wait here." He started to walk away but then thought better of it, and turned back to face her. "No, instead—come with me."

They walked out a side door and into the garden. He was rewarded by the young woman's gasp of delight. She looked up at him with expectation. "Explore as much as you wish. I will return in a moment," he told her before returning to the house.

Once in the study, he paced for a few minutes before opening the envelope and pulling out the thin sheet of expensive paper within.

Grant darling,

It has been days since you have seen me. I am in despair over your absence.

   Come immediately. We must talk.

   I yearn for you.

Lucinda

Grant crumpled the paper and blew out a breath. If not for the fact the woman was about to pay for a venture that would secure his independence by making him rich, he'd not reply at all.

Walking over to the fireplace, he tossed the paper into the fire and watched as the flames consumed it. How easy it would be to walk away at this point. To not continue to put up with Lucinda's need for constant attention.

How he yearned for a strong, independent woman. His sister Felicity was a prime example of a woman who was self-reliant and an equal decision-maker with her husband, Evan. Then there was his friend Henry's wife, who'd managed a household and all that had to be done in spite of and following her father's murder and mother's abandonment.

Lucinda, on the other hand, was as helpless as a babe, requiring a team of maids, accountants, assistants, and lovers to see to her every need. Attention was like air to her.

Knowing he had to reply, he went to the desk and pulled out a piece of paper, then dipped the quill into the ink and found he could not formulate any words.

Finally, he wrote one single sentence:

Lucinda,

I will visit today.

Grant

He stared at the single line. How had his life come to this? As much as he claimed to wish for an independent woman, he was no better than Lucinda. His lovers fed him, dressed him, and ensured that he had all that a gentleman required. Without any money of his own, he depended on finding wealthy lovers in exchange for the luxurious lifestyle to which he'd become accustomed.

"Sir?" Norman came to the door. "Did ye forget about the lass? Should I offer her a refreshment?"

"Grand idea, Norman," Grant said. "Bring tea out to the garden. I will eat with the young lady who is here to deliver a message that I am not sure how to reply to."

The butler gave him a puzzled look. "You do realize she is a servant?"

"Is she?" Grant had not thought about it. "Ah, yes, you are probably right."

"So would you prefer to have your tea indoors?" Norman asked, his face a study in how to not express what one thinks.

Grant shrugged. "No, I will have my tea in the garden with the little maid. I have questions for her, and I am quite hungry."

"As you wish." Norman walked away, and Grant followed. Instead of taking the note with him, he placed it on a side table. For some reason, he was anxious to get outside to discover what the maid's reaction to the garden was. There would be time to return inside and retrieve the note to give to her. For the moment, he preferred to pretend a young woman had come to call on him and that they would have a delightful meal together. After all, there was nothing else to do with his time.

However, if he was to procure the money from Lucinda, he had to ensure he was not to be seen with anyone else. As it was, since his full attention was being taken by Lucinda, his other lovers were growing impatient at his lack of time for them. So soon, he'd start doing less with her. Very soon.

The two women that he visited regularly, twice monthly, had both sent invitations that he'd been forced to not accept. In truth, it was becoming annoying; it was as if he was indeed losing as much of his freedom as Evan and Henry in spite of the fact he was still unmarried.

Although Grant wished to do as he pleased, at the moment, the most important thing was the money for the ship. Therefore, Lucinda had to be his priority.

He caught his reflection in a large mirror and leaned in closer. His eyes were clear despite staying up late the night before. His hair was a bit disheveled, and his cravat was loose. A true rogue depended on his looks, which combined with impeccable grooming were a perfect enticement to a possible lover.

At the moment, however, there was no seduction planned and no need to be looking his best. All it would be was tea with a young woman, one who didn't aspire to anything more than the chance to enjoy the garden.

His lips curved in a smile. For the first time in a long time, he looked forward to time spent with a woman, one who would not demand anything from him. Instead, she would in all probability, be more interested in the surroundings than in flirting with him.

It was a liberating feeling.

CHAPTER TWO

W REN DARROW BENT at the waist to sniff the large lilac-like flower and wondered what it was. She'd never seen so many varieties of flora in her life. As much as she enjoyed gardening, she'd always planted and cultivated vegetables to put food on the table. A floral garden was a treat, something to be enjoyed, and most people like her did not have the luxury of growing one.

New to Glasgow, she'd gone directly to her Aunt Mairid's home located in the city. Narrow streets wound around buildings built too closely together; one could reach and touch two structures at the same time. It left little room for growing things, and the bit of dirt that was available to her aunt had already been planted with only tomatoes and cooking herbs, that she could tell.

Moving from the country had been a shock to her senses; however, walking through this garden was a welcome reprieve. The mingling fragrances of flowers reminded her of her child-hood spent in the country chasing butterflies in fields filled with wildflowers.

Wren stole a glance toward the house. The astonishingly handsome gentleman had yet to reappear.

Strange this task she'd been assigned, with no other instruc-tion than to deliver the note and then wait for a reply.

Thanks to her aunt, who'd worked for Lady Roberts for many years, she'd been able to get her a placement in the household. In the short time she'd worked for Lady Roberts, she'd not been in the walled-off garden at the estate. Although she'd spied some flowers from where she hung clothes to dry, she hadn't seen more than a few patches of green most days because she was usually inside with her aunt.

Still, as of yet, Wren had not been assigned a specific position, which was a bit unsettling. In truth, it had been strange. Even on the day she'd arrived, the household had been in chaos. Apparently, there had been a huge party and many of those who'd attended had remained overnight. The morning after, most left hurriedly, not bothering with staff and seeming to wish to flee rather than remain and break their fast.

When she'd asked her aunt about the goings-on, she'd been told to hush and not ask any questions.

"Better to be ignorant of the facts than to be pulled into gossip," her aunt had said.

She'd continued to show up at the estate each day where, other than being given odd jobs here and there, Wren had yet to be placed. So when the mistress had asked for someone not busy to take a message, she'd been the one sent.

Looking around the perfectly-tended garden, Wren realized she was alone for the first time in many days. Her heartbeat had yet to slow. It was the first time she'd gone off on her own since arriving just one week earlier.

There was no real reason to feel unsettled, and nothing seemed amiss. But the ride in the carriage had given her an opportunity to see more of Glasgow, and the sights had made her head spin. The city was huge, colorful, and absolutely beautiful. Perhaps that was what was making her heart race. It was just seeing how large the city was, and knowing she'd only seen but a portion of it.

She'd grown up in a small village north of the city. Overall, Wren had had a good life. However, all had changed after her parents and sister caught the pox and died, one right after the other. Left alone and without means to make a living, Wren had been relieved when her aunt insisted Wren return to Glasgow with her. Now she wondered how on earth she could ever fit into such a large place.

So far life had been simple. Her Aunt Mairid was widowed and had a son, Lars, who was married and lived closer to the city center. He had several shops and provided well for his family. Aunt Mairid had told her that on occasion, her cousin Lars and his wife and children would visit. Her aunt's house was a comfortable, small home, attached to three others, two up and two down. She lived on the bottom floor. Her small bedroom was cozy.

She worked during the day and came home with her aunt to enjoy a meal, do a few chores, and then go to bed early. Though she'd kept the same hours as she had at home, in Glasgow, life was quite different than life on the farm where she'd grown up. Everything they needed had to be purchased.

Now, Wren straightened and looked toward the doorway. Interesting that the man had yet to return. Torn with what to do, she went out through a gate and walked to the carriage. The driver was leaning back, eyes closed.

"Excuse me," Wren whispered.

The man straightened and frowned down at her. "Ready to leave?"

"No, he told me to wait in the garden and has yet to return. What should I do?"

He gave her an incredulous look. "Hurry, go back. Do not be daft. Wait for him. If it takes hours, you wait."

Chastised, she rushed back to the garden and looked around. There was no one about, giving her freedom to explore. In actuality, it was a wonderful respite from doing laundry or scrubbing floors at the Roberts mansion. So she didn't mind at all.

Wren wandered to an area where there was a table and chairs. She studied the furniture, wondering if it was appropriate for her to sit. Finally she picked a seat from which she could see the door and be aware of the gentleman exiting so she could stand as soon as he appeared.

Once seated, she let out a sigh. Whoever lived here probably took such a wonderful place for granted. She would never. Not that she could ever aspire to such a life. A light breeze blew across the garden, the perfumed air caressing her skin. Unable to keep herself from enjoying the sensation, she stood, lifted her face to the sun, and inhaled deeply. This was a moment she'd treasured for a long time. Eyes still closed, she lifted her hands up, as if to embrace the sun.

"What exactly are you doing?" The deep voice made her make a surprised yelp, and she jumped so high that her sturdy shoes tapped on the flat stone when she landed.

"I—I apologize, Mr. Grant... er...Murray. I was smelling the flowers." Her face felt as if it had been burned by the sun she'd just been worshipping.

Grant Murray was the most handsome man she'd ever seen. When he'd first appeared, her breath had caught, and Wren was sure she'd gawked. Thankfully, he'd not seemed to notice.

At this moment, however, his brown gaze was steady on her, as if trying to figure out if she was feeble-minded. "I see." He looked to the nearest flowers. "You seem quite fond of the garden."

Unable to keep from doing so, she smiled widely. "I am."

"Norman is bringing tea. I hope you will join me, Miss..."

"Darrow, Wren Darrow," she replied. "I couldn't possibly. I am sure Lady Roberts would not approve."

"Probably not. However, I am famished and hate eating alone." He motioned to the same chair she'd been sitting on, and she wondered if he'd seen her perched there, however briefly it had been.

Wren edged closer to the chair but didn't sit. "If you could give me your reply, I will take it to her and be out of your way."

"I do not have a reply as yet," he stated, then went to the chair, pulled it back, and motioned for her to sit.

Feeling awkward and horribly underdressed, Wren sat and looked down at her chipped nails.

When he lowered his broad form into a chair across from her, she could sense his gaze on her. "I do not believe I've seen you before."

She shook her head. "I only just arrived in Glasgow. My aunt works for Lady Roberts. With my aunt's help, I was able to get employment at the house." Lifting her gaze, she noted he looked away from her.

"Where did you come from then?"

"North of here, a small village, Bearsden."

He nodded as if he knew the place. Wren didn't dare ask him any questions, and after a moment's pause, he said, "I have been through there. My father has family near there. Have you heard of Milngavie? Many have not."

She couldn't keep from nodding enthusiastically. "I have. My parents and I often went there for their harvest festival."

"Ah, yes. Quite the thing." Her companion met her gaze. "We may have been there at the same time in the past."

She doubted that. Certainly, she'd remember such a handsome man, even if she'd seen him at a distance or in a crowd.

A clearing of the throat was followed by an austere butler and a maid nearing. They placed the tea service on the table, followed by two plates, each with a meal of sliced pieces of meat, roasted potatoes, and a chunk of bread.

"Do you require anything else, sir?" the butler asked, his expression unreadable.

"No, that will be all. Thank you, Norman."

Before Wren could reach for the pot, Grant took it and poured tea for both of them. "I appreciate your company. Thank you for staying."

It wasn't as if she had a choice. Nonetheless, it was kind of him to thank her.

"Of course, sir."

THEY ATE IN silence for a few moments, and Grant was sure the poor woman hoped to be allowed to leave. He almost told her she could, but then she smiled widely, and all thought left him.

"Look!" She pointed to a bluebird that lighted on a nearby branch, and she whispered to it, "Aren't you a handsome one?"

This was a woman who took joy in the simple things. When he'd walked out and caught her in that stirring pose, he'd wished to be a painter in order to immortalize the sight. She was quite a beauty. Not like the elegant, overdone women he escorted, but in the simple, breath-of-fresh-air kind of way.

Wren had large, expressive eyes that were adorned with long lashes. Her face was kissed by the sun, a sprinkling of freckles across her pert nose. Her mouth was a bit large for her face, but it added to her allure. When he'd walked into the garden to see her with her arms outstretched to the sun, with an expression of pure joy, she'd been the most beautiful thing he'd seen in a long time.

"Why have you not replied to Lady Robert's note?" She'd stopped eating and sipped from the cup, her ragged fingernails a contrast to the delicate item.

"I am not sure what to say," Grant replied honestly. "I cannot tell her the truth because I know it will anger her. So, I must reply in a way that will not upset her."

Wren's brow lowered. "Quite a quandary then."

"It is." He shrugged. "In truth, I did write something. But I am not sure if it is the correct response." Grant wasn't sure why he was confessing to a servant. However, she was an impartial party, and it was obvious she had no idea of the relationship which existed between him and Lucinda.

"You should always be honest. People appreciate honesty," Wren said. "Is she your aunt? A relation?"

Instead of a reply, he looked at the flowers. "You should pick some of those for yourself. I am sure there are shears about here somewhere."

By the slight lift at the corners of her lips, Wren appeared to understand he'd diverted the subject to keep from answering her question. "I would love to."

Her gaze met his for just a split second, but it was long enough for him to notice the rare color of her eyes. They were a light blue, with specks of a darker blue shade. Combined with her auburn hair and freckled nose, she was a rare treat to the senses.

"Are you married?" Grant wasn't sure why he'd blurted the question, other than because he did wonder if she was truly as innocent as she seemed.

Immediately she stiffened, her gaze flying to where the carriage awaited. He'd scared her, and Grant wanted to kick himself for it. "Forget the question. It is none of my affair."

She relaxed visibly. "I will see about choosing a few flowers."

"Of course." Grant went to the small garden shed and upon finding shears brought them to Wren. "There you are. I will return shortly with my reply for Lady Roberts."

Once inside the house, he paced. He didn't wish to visit Lucinda. It would be the first time visiting since he'd had an incident with Tom Roberts, her son, and he did not look forward to Lucinda's chastisement. Perhaps he could claim feeling unwell. "No," he said out loud. "I should visit."

Grant grunted and stared down at the envelope he'd placed on the table. He picked it up and went to find Wren.

Holding just three flowers, she hurried to him and held them up for inspection. "They are beautiful. Thank you so very much." At the delight on her face, Grant wanted to gift her the entire garden. Acres and acres of flowers would not be worth her delighted smile.

"Thank you for sharing a meal with me," he replied, returning her smile.

"It is I who should thank you, sir. I have not had such a wonderful meal in a long time." Wren plucked the envelope from his fingers and practically danced toward the gate and the carriage waiting beyond.

Moments later, it ambled down the drive and out of sight.

CHAPTER THREE

"LASS. GET UP. We must leave soon," her aunt called from the kitchen.

Wren woke from a deep sleep, sat up, and stretched. The first thing she saw was the vase holding the beautiful flowers she'd brought back from her errand the day before. How she wished they'd last forever, not only because they were beautiful, but because they were a reminder of one of the most delight-filled days in her twenty-one years.

Walking in the beautiful garden, the flowers, the birds, and the delicious meal were wonderful, but the best part of all was to have shared it with a handsome man who'd been so kind. Unsurprisingly, she'd dreamed of him, of sharing another moment in the garden.

This time, he'd taken her hand and they'd danced to a beautiful melody.

Wren giggled at the thought. That a maid had shared a meal with a gentleman was unbelievable. Even if she dared to tell it to someone, they would never believe her. It was the stuff of dreams.

Now, it was barely light outside, the sun still low in the sky. She slipped from the bed and yawned widely. Her aunt always rose quite early, breaking her fast and spending time in prayer. Wren understood she needed the time alone, which suited her fine as she appreciated the extra time to sleep.

Once dressed and with her hair braided, Wren donned her

cap and apron. Then she went to the kitchen where she ate a simple meal of porridge and toasted bread.

"There is much to do today," her aunt informed her. "You will be helping to weed the garden and prepare herbs for drying. I told the headmistress of your penchant for gardening."

"Is that to be my position?" Wren asked, smiling. "Gardening?"

"For now, aye," her aunt said. "I hope to secure you a place as a chambermaid, otherwise, you will be exposed to the elements, and all that bending cannot be good."

Wren wasn't particularly worried. Although it would be troublesome to be outdoors when the weather became cooler, for now, she was grateful to have work, and she would do what was needed.

LATER THAT MORNING, along with a young lad, Wren followed an old man named Rufus to the garden.

"We will start here." He poked his walking stick into the soil and then used it as he shuffled to the edge of the plantings and pointed with it. "And go to here." Wren hurried to catch up, while the lad with them crossed his arms looking bored.

Rufus frowned down at her. "Do you know the difference between good plants, herbs, and weeds?"

"I do," Wren replied, lowering to point at a plant with branches that had leaves made out of tinier ones. "This is Sweet Cicely. Good for cough and other ailments." She pinched a leaf and sniffed it. "Sweet."

The old man did not seem impressed. "Very well then, go ahead. Keep the lad in line. He is called Tim." He walked off without providing further instructions.

Of all the jobs, she would have preferred to work in the kitchen. As much as she loved gardens and the outdoors, Wren had never quite mastered cooking, and working in the kitchen would have given her ample opportunities to gain experience.

Before the death of her family, her mother and sister had done all the cooking, and she had been expected to tend to the garden, which admittedly was much harder work compared to cooking. But now, she wondered if she'd even be successfully able to boil water, an important life skill.

For his part, Tim didn't bother pretending to work. Instead, he kicked a rock against the garden wall, over and over, while she tugged weeds.

"Fetch me the wheelbarrow, please?" Wren asked Tim, not bothering to look at him. She gathered by his expression and constant looks toward the stables, he'd hoped to work with the horses instead of in the garden. The lad seemed startled by her kind tone. But she didn't feel resentment at his lack of participation in their assigned labor.

"Aye, very well." His head bobbed and then he hurried off in the direction of the stables, making her wonder if he'd ever return. As she watched him go, a man on horseback arrived in the stable yard and dismounted.

She straightened, leaning back on her heels to look at him. The shade from his hat didn't allow her to see his face, but by his build and hair color, she was certain it was Grant Murray. Thankfully, he couldn't see her as she was on the side of the house behind a wall. Though, even if he did spot her, it was probable he'd pretend not to know her.

Once the horse was taken, he strolled toward the house. With long strides, he cut a fine figure in his riding attire, complete with a calf-long overcoat and knee-high riding boots. In one gloved hand, he carried a parcel. Almost as if sensing her perusal, Grant hesitated and turned, but he didn't seem to notice her hidden behind the wall as she was.

Either that, or he thought her only to be a curious member of the household staff, which indeed she was. She knew she shouldn't—and couldn't—expect him to speak to her in a friendly fashion, in spite of how they'd shared a meal the morning before. But that didn't mean she didn't feel a tinge of disappointment. Obviously, their interaction meant far less to him than it did to her, and reasonably so.

Once at the front steps, the butler opened the doors and Grant disappeared into the house.

Sounds got her attention and she turned to find the lad heading over, pushing the wheelbarrow whilst another followed behind him, yelling.

"What happened?" Wren got to her feet and met them at the garden gate.

"He must return the wheelbarrow to me," the lad who'd come up behind Tim informed her. "He just grabbed it from my hands."

Tim, who seemed to have mastered a bored expression, looked at her but answered the other young man, "I was told to bring a wheelbarrow."

Oh dear. She hadn't meant to cause a ruckus. "If it's not convenient for me to use a wheelbarrow, perhaps you have a bucket or something else," Wren told the red-faced lad. "There's no need to be angry."

The boy snatched the handles from Tim and hurried away, pushing the wheelbarrow in front of him.

"What now?" Tim asked, looking after where the other lad went. "A bucket?"

Wren nodded, and he went to a small shed and pointed. "There are plenty in there."

He expected her to fetch it herself? And do all the weeding as well? Why was he even here? Wren gave him a pointed look, and he let out a breath and went into the shed, emerging with two buckets. He then placed them where she motioned. "Pull these," Wren instructed, pointing at a bright green, tendril-like weed that had done its best to overtake the garden. To her surprise, Tim kneeled and began yanking the plants, then tossing them into the bucket.

Once again, she got onto her knees and started working, the entire time wondering what occurred inside. Was Mr. Grant to be a guest for more than one day? What exactly was his relationship with her employer?

"I hear you need a wheelbarrow," a masculine voice right behind her startled Wren. It was one of the men who worked with the livestock. He was probably her age, with a youthful plumpness to his face and a cheerful look about him. "I am Albert. I brought this wheelbarrow." He motioned unnecessarily to the item. "Do you need me to take whatever you will put into it away?"

So far, she and Tim filled two buckets with weeds and had begun to just pile more on the ground. "Oh, thank you. No need. Tim can do it."

Tim, who'd grown bored with the task of lazily plucking a weed here and there, came out of his stupor and walked to Albert. "I will do it. I can take the weeds to be burned." Then Tim looked at her, and it was obvious he expected her to put them into the wheelbarrow.

Wren had had enough. "Put all of this into there." She pointed. "Have care lest you get a scratch on your soft hands."

Tim lost his permanently bored expression and sneered. Albert laughed. "Aye, our Tim is not one for hard work."

"Or any work if you ask me," Wren said, satisfied to see Tim doing as told.

Albert winked at her and walked away whistling, past a maid who glared in her direction. It occurred to her that she would have to learn who to get to know and who to avoid.

"WREN." HER AUNT appeared at the edge of the garden later that afternoon. "You must be famished."

Wren realized she'd not eaten since the morning and indeed,

she was quite hungry. She got up and followed her aunt, stopping at the well to draw some water so she could wash the garden dirt from her hands. Then, they ate in the kitchen at a small table in the corner while the cook and maids worked around them with quick efficiency.

Wren leaned closer to her aunt. "The stableman named Albert brought a wheelbarrow and talked to me. As he returned, I noticed there was a maid who was not happy about it."

Her aunt sniffed. "Do not bother with them. There is always something going on between the lasses and the lads who work here. Best to keep to yourself and not worry about such things."

It wasn't exactly what she wanted to know, but it didn't matter. The last thing she was interested in was any kind of entanglement. Wren's priority was to work hard and make money so that she could help her aunt with expenses. But there was one thing that interested her about the household, and she couldn't help but ask, "The man, Mr. Murray, is he related to Lady Roberts?"

At this, the kitchen maid snickered, then quieted when the cook gave her a stern look. Her aunt's cheeks pinkened. "He is a friend of the family." She changed the subject abruptly. "Finish your chores promptly. I wish to go home and have enough time to help out at the vicarage."

Lucinda was uncharacteristically undemonstrative and lacking in any sort of excitement at his arrival. Usually, the woman would greet him with her hands outstretched for him to take in his.

Pretending not to notice, he leaned over and pressed a kiss to both her cheeks and then lowered into a chair across from the settee in which she sat. Dressed in a pale lavender gown that would have been better suited for someone a quarter of her age, hair pulled up in a youthful arrangement, and cheeks stained with rouge, the woman fought hard to remain young. Unfortunately, her attempts to appear youthful usually had the opposite effect. Today, she appeared pale and sallow in the sunlight that shined through the window.

For months, he'd chosen to ignore her appearance, pretending to find the woman attractive. And it was true that, from portraits on the walls, she had been quite attractive when she was younger. Perhaps because of this, she had married three times. But it didn't stop her from being widowed. After the last husband, with both Lord Roberts and her youthful appearance gone, she'd remained a widow. The now-departed Lord had left the bulk of his fortune to Lucinda, making her a wealthy woman. So instead of remarrying and chancing the loss of that wealth, she'd taken lover after lover.

Grant was her latest.

A maid entered and poured tea. Plump scones and jam were placed on plates before them.

"Have Rufus come see me," Lucinda told the maid. The young woman nodded and hurried away. Grant speculated how, anytime young women were near, Lucinda watched him like a hawk. Truly, he considered it comical, as he was well-versed in how to make a woman feel as if she was the only one who mattered. Even if he noticed someone who took his attention, he made sure to keep his observations discreet.

"Where have you been?" Lucinda asked without preamble. "You must know we must discuss what occurred between you and my son."

He mulled over how to best reply. "His attack was unprovoked. As you can imagine, I was unprepared and defended myself by hitting him. I am told he is unharmed."

"He is." Lucinda's eyes narrowed. "I do not see a mar on your face. A blessing, I am sure."

After a discreet knock, an older man with muddied boots stood at the doorway. It was shocking to see Lucinda's expression relax at seeing the man. "The garden outside this window. I would like to ensure the flowers are pruned so that they are bright and colorful in a fortnight."

The man nodded, looking past them to the window. "The new lass, she seems knowledgeable of plants. I will have her work there instead of the herb garden."

Lucinda waved his words away impatiently. "I do not care how you do it, just ensure it is done." Then she met the old man's gaze for a moment. "It may require more than just one lass. You should help." She paused, then asked, "Who is this lass?"

Rufus motioned behind himself to someone out of sight, and Wren appeared. Unlike the time before when she'd delivered a message to him, she wore a dirty apron, and her hair was tucked under a straw hat. Thankfully, she kept her gaze down. and he prayed she would not say anything to alert Lucinda that they'd met before.

"Lass, what do you know about flora?" Lucinda asked.

Wren lifted her gaze just enough to look at her mistress and then back to the floor. "I worked with my family growing vegetables, and we had a lush flower garden, my lady."

Not surprisingly, Lucinda did not seem impressed. "Ensure not to do any damage to my precious flowers. Some are imported and require much care."

Wren's head bobbed. "Yes, my lady."

"Go on then." Lucinda turned her attention back to Rufus. "I trust you will keep an eye on her."

Bobbing a quick curtsy, it was then that Wren finally looked at him. Her gaze remained flat and without recognition, as if she didn't remember him. Then she turned and followed the old man out of the room.

"Her aunt, who's been with me for many years, asked me to take the lass on. I am glad that she will be of some use in the garden. My only other choice would be to send her to work with the hogs." Lucinda's unkind words made him flinch. All of the women on Lucinda's staff were plain, some outright ugly, and it occurred to Grant that the older, vain woman had developed an automatic dislike of younger, pretty women, not wishing to be outshined.

Lucinda picked up a scone and took a dainty bite. "Back to the subject at hand. My son insists that you are only interested in me because of my money. I do not disagree. I know you can have any woman you please. However, I am a bit disconcerted that after that unpleasant episode, you did not come to explain yourself."

His heart raced. Was the woman about to take back her offer to pay for his portion of the ship sponsorship? It was time to pull every weapon from his arsenal and ensure he used them wisely.

Grant moved to sit next to her, taking her hand in both of his. "I did plan to come and speak to you. However, I was not sure you would welcome my visit. He is your son, and I should have refrained from hitting him. I beg you to accept my heartfelt apologies."

Lucinda sniffed with annoyance. "It is him you should be apologizing to. He is quite put out."

It proved almost impossible not to clench his jaw. "I will make every effort to seek him out and…"

"He said he saw you at The Grant and that you made no effort to seek him out there. Quite the contrary, in fact."

"Lucinda. I cannot undo the past. I did not apologize because as I have explained, he attacked me."

"He defended his mother's honor."

"Very true, and it is commendable." In truth, he despised the pompous man and wished he'd hit him a few more times.

"That goes without saying. My Tom is very protective of me."

Being that Tom rarely visited his mother, didn't stand with her at events, and didn't even have anything to do with Lucinda's care, Grant discerned that what Tom was protective of was his mother's fortune.

"Of course," he replied noncommittally. He had absolutely

no plans to apologize to the idiot. Hopefully, it would be a short time before a ball or social engagement would take greater precedence in Lucinda's mind.

"Now," Lucinda said, lifting a dainty cup to her lips. "You are to escort me to an event tomorrow evening." Her gaze skimmed from his booted feet and over his body to finally meet his gaze. "See about presentable attire. Also, go to the tailor. He has instructions as to what you will be wearing to the spring gala next week." Her voice lowered to a secretive tone. "As Tom has begun visiting unannounced, meet me at my townhouse tonight. Eight o'clock sharp."

Something akin to nausea rose within Grant. It wasn't new that he slept with various women in exchange for a rather lavish lifestyle. It was just that this time, Lucinda ordered his movements and wardrobe, and he had no choice in the matter. It was not the kind of arrangement he usually made.

However, there was the matter of the huge sum she'd promised, and the woman was aware he would not rebel against anything she asked until the money was securely in his account.

"Very well." He managed a smile. "I am glad that you are not so upset as to deny me your company."

Movement from outside caught his attention. Wren appeared carrying a large, rustic basket, her pretty face shaded by the rather tattered straw hat she wore. She looked up to the sky, her lips curving, and he almost smiled but quickly looked to Lucinda, whose eyes had narrowed as she observed his attention on the young woman.

"Why do you need the garden to be prepared in a fortnight?" He scrambled to come up with a reason for his study of the garden.

"I am hosting a lady's tea there. The last one was hosted by Catriona Campbell, whose garden is without fault. Once the girl and Rufus get mine started, I am going to hire a professional team to ensure mine is much grander."

Grant wanted to roll his eyes. Lucinda rarely paid any mind

to flowers or the like. Her preferred pursuits took place indoors. Her circle of friends were older members of high society who were brought together by their fight against aging. Instead of enjoying their elderly status, they'd turned to pursuits that bordered on perversion.

Unfortunately, as Lucinda's lover, he was part of that life-style—for the moment.

Letting out a sigh, he stood. "As much as I'd like to stay, I must go. I have an appointment with Lord Johnstone," he lied. "He values promptness, so I do not wish to be late."

"Of course, darling," Lucinda held up a hand for him to kiss. "I look forward to our time together tonight."

CHAPTER FOUR

A T THE END of the day, the garden was weeded, and the new
plants both she and Rufus had planted were mulched. The
entire section just outside the window would be bright with color
once all the buds bloomed.

Wren nipped a few more leaves away from the soon-to-be-
bright flowers and dropped the clippers into her basket. She let
out a sigh and stretched her back. As much as she enjoyed
gardening, it was not work for the physically weak.

Tapping on the window, Lady Roberts got her attention. The
woman motioned for her to come closer.

She had to push the basket aside with one foot to move to the
now-open window and she peered up. In the sunlight, Lady
Roberts' skin was pale, and the wrinkles around her eyes and
corners of her mouth were much more obvious as well. "What
are those?" She pointed a spindly finger at the plant she'd just
trimmed.

"Dahlias, my lady."

"Can you move them? They are growing quite tall and will
block my view of the drive." The woman put a handkerchief up
to her nose. "It is quite potent out here. What is that dreadful
smell?"

Wren looked behind her, unsure what question to reply to
first. "If we move the flowers, they will wilt and die. The smell is
cow dung that Rufus mixed with soil to fertilize the garden." She
realized she had not addressed the woman properly and belatedly

added, "...My lady."

The woman glared down at her. "Go fetch that man and ask him to see me immediately. And trim down those horrid flowers. I do not see any blooms."

"My lady, they will bloom into beautiful, brightly-colored flowers in less than a sennight."

Lady Roberts' narrowed eyes moved from the small buds to her. "Oh, very well, leave them for now." For a long moment, she studied her. "Stay away from my window whenever I have a caller."

"Yes, milady," Wren answered, doubting Lady Roberts heard as she'd slammed the window shut. The woman was not kind, which she'd expected. Her aunt had warned her that Lady Roberts was peculiar and not very well-liked by the servants. Most tolerated her because they needed work and that, in spite of her rather unpleasant disposition, Lady Roberts paid well.

After fetching an annoyed Rufus and sending him on his mission, Wren filled a bucket with water and rinsed the dirt from her hands and forearms. Once satisfied to have removed all the dirt including that from under her fingernails, she drew more water and splashed it on her face. In the small shed where garden items were kept, she hung the straw hat and dirty apron on a nail before she finally retrieved her kerchief and placed it on her head, tying it under her chin. Then she went inside the house.

In the kitchen, a bowl of stew and a piece of bread awaited her on the long sturdy table where they often gathered for meals and to be given instructions in the morning by the butler and Berta.

The cook gave her a patient smile. "You should come and eat earlier next time. There is no need to work so hard for so long. Our work is rarely noticed by anyone in this household." The woman held out a cup of cider.

"I was right outside the window where Lady Roberts sat. I was afraid to leave." Wren accepted the cider with a chuckle.

The cook nodded. "That is understandable."

Just then Rufus entered. "Daft woman," he muttered. "Who has nae heard of fertilizer?"

The cook shook her head. "One of these days she will overhear you and put you out."

"Let her try," Rufus retorted. He took the cup of cider she offered and drank it down in several gulps. Then he lowered himself onto a bench at the table where Wren ate. "I am nae cuttin' the flowers. Neither are you." He held up a gnarled finger. "You hear me, lass?"

Wren nodded solemnly.

With that, he stood and stalked out.

"Those two are always at odds," the cook said. "Lady Roberts and Rufus grew up together here at the estate. Before Rufus, his father was the gardener."

"Does Rufus have a son who will take over for him?" Wren asked, noting that the cook went still, her gaze moving in the direction that Rufus had gone.

"No." She turned away to stir a pot. "A pity."

Just then two kitchen maids entered, giggling and talking excitingly. Their young faces were brightly flushed. The cook gave them a knowing look. "Wren, be sure not to be like these two," she said, motioning with her right thumb. "They spend their breaks flirting with the footmen."

The maids paid her no heed and continued whispering. All the while, Wren envied their friendship and ability to enjoy life's moments. She'd yet to make a friend.

On the ride home with her aunt, she brought up the subject. "When two kitchen maids returned from their break, chattering, I realized that I haven't made any friends," she lamented.

Her aunt gave her a knowing look. "You have me."

"And I do adore you, Aunt Mairid, but I wish to meet someone my age to do things with."

"Well, there are plenty of young lasses at the house. Also, you haven't had the opportunity to meet anyone in the area in which we live. I am sure you will soon find a friend." Her aunt smiled.

"Speaking of which, I must stop and visit Martha, she has not been feeling well at all."

When the wagon stopped, both Wren and her aunt climbed down. Her aunt waved in the direction of where they lived. "Continue on to the house. I will see about Martha and be home shortly."

"I will start supper," Wren said as they came to the small house where Martha lived, and her aunt went to the front door. Wren continued to their home, which was not very far, where she took the shopping basket that had been left by the door and continued on the short distance to the village center.

The square was bustling with activity. It was the end of the day, and most were there to gather items to cook for dinner. She went to the bakers and purchased a loaf of bread, then stopped at a stall and purchased sausages. Once that was done, she turned to head back home.

A man stepped in front of her, his dark gaze taking her in. "Do I know you?"

Wren moved backward, not liking how close he was. "No, I do not think so." She took a step sideways. "Allow me to pass, sir."

"I think I know you," the man persisted. He was a bit taller than her, and of stocky build, reminding her of an ox. He had a thick neck, dark brown hair, and a bushy beard. "Ah yes, you came to my father's shop the other day. With your aunt."

Unable to remember him, but hoping that he'd allow her past, Wren nodded. "That must be it."

He crossed his beefy arms. "You're new here. I can show you around." When the corners of his lips curved, Wren felt an urge to kick him. A man did not court a woman by intimidating her.

"It is not necessary. My aunt has shown me the entire area." It was not an exaggeration since the small village on the outskirts of Glasgow was not particularly large. "If you would excuse me, she is expecting me at home."

"I am Clyde," he said as if she'd not spoken a word, and then gave her an expectant look.

"My name is Wren." She took a second sideways step. "I best be on my way."

It wasn't surprising when Clyde came alongside, his bulky form walking in sync with her. "I will ensure you arrive home safely then."

"I can see my house from here," Wren said dryly. "There is no need."

He stopped and touched her forearm. "If I can be of assistance, do not hesitate to ask." His earnest expression made Wren relax.

"Very well, Clyde. Thank you."

Wren continued home, shaking her head. She'd asked for a girlfriend, not a butcher's son who was also, apparently, an admirer. A few moments later, she sifted the dirt in her aunt's small garden, looking to unearth some potatoes to go with the sausage, when a young woman appeared from the square and walked up the path leading to the house where she stopped.

"Are you Wren?" she asked and smiled, displaying a gap between her front teeth. "I am Laurel. Your Aunt Mairid sent me to tell you she will not be coming home for supper."

Alarmed, Wren left the garden and hurried to stand near Laurel. "Did something happen to her?"

"No," Laurel said, shaking her head. "My Aunt Martha invited her to remain. They sent me to come for you to join us."

"Oh. I did not know Martha had someone living with her," Wren replied, delighted to meet Laurel, who seemed to have a sunny disposition.

"I have moved in with her during the last sennight. She has been rather poorly and my mother, her sister, asked if I could help care for her." Laurel waited as Wren put the items she had purchased inside their house and locked the front door. They walked side-by-side to Martha's house.

The young woman continued her chatter. "Of course, I do not mind. I have two sisters and a brother still at home, which makes our house rather crowded. At Aunt Martha's, I have my own bedroom. It is quite delightful. I wish I would have thought of it sooner."

"As you may know, I recently arrived to live with my aunt as well," Wren said. "She tells me that your mother, your aunt, and she are childhood friends."

"Thick as thieves, they are," Laurel exclaimed. When the young woman wove her arm through hers as they walked, Wren smiled.

It was turning out to be quite an interesting day.

CHAPTER FIVE

T HE SUN WAS barely up when Grant made his way back home the following morning. Unfortunately, Lucinda had not mentioned anything about the money, and he was becoming frustrated. Having spent the day before at the tailor's and then at the barbershop where Lucinda had ordered his hair to be cut a certain way, his nails manicured, and even that he be given a precise shave, he'd been in a sour mood when arriving at the townhouse.

By the time he and Lucinda had eaten dinner, he'd drunk three glasses of whiskey and was well into his fourth. Needless to say, he barely remembered if there had been any activity once they'd gone to bed. Now, through bleary eyes, he noted a lone woman with a basket hanging from her arm, who didn't seem to hear him approach.

"Wren?"

She whirled around and stared up at him with wide eyes, seeming disconcerted for a moment before her lips spread into a smile. "Mr. Murray. You are out and about quite early."

"I am heading—" he was about to say "home", but decided it was best not to infer he'd been out all night, especially at her employer's home, or in her bed—"Out for a ride."

If she noticed his disheveled appearance, she didn't show it. Instead, she nodded. "A perfect morning for it, sir."

Dismounting, he walked alongside her. "And where are you off to so early?"

The basket swayed when she held her arm out. "To the market to purchase a few items for the cook at Lady Robert's estate. She is very picky about things and wishes for items to make a special dish."

"Ah," Grant was grateful for the picky cook. "I will accompany you there and give you a ride back. It is a bit of a walk."

"Oh, do not trouble yourself, sir. It is a nice morning. I do not mind."

He looked off into the distance. "That is quite a long walk."

"Not much longer than our walks to the estate some mornings," she quipped, keeping her brisk pace.

"Your aunt walks from your home and back each day?"

Wren laughed. "At times. Most mornings we ride in a wagon, with others who travel to and from the estate."

"I insist on taking you there." Grant wasn't sure how he could deliver the lass without being seen, but he could not possibly allow her to walk so far.

Now he remained at a distance as Wren walked from stall to stall, purchasing what was needed. A man at one of the stands was overly cheerful when Wren approached, seeming to give her quite a bit of attention. The attention was not surprising, as she was lovely and had a welcoming personality.

When she finally walked toward him, her face was bright.

"Let us get you to work," Grant said, taking her by the waist and hoisting her up to the horse. He then lifted the basket up to her and finally mounted, awkwardly taking the reins while avoiding the cumbersome basket.

"Goodness, this is quite high," Wren said, peering down at the ground. She squirmed a bit, not seeming to realize that by doing so she rubbed against the area between his legs. Grant swallowed and was thankful for his hangover. His throbbing temples distracted him enough not to become aroused.

They rode for a short distance without speaking. It was enjoyable to have the lass so close. He'd never ridden like this before, with a woman between his legs. In the city, it would be frowned upon, but as they rode through the villages, life was not only simpler but also less complicated with fewer rules of etiquette and proper behavior.

Sitting sideways, Wren clutched the basket handle to her chest. "Do you often ride in the early mornings?"

Grant looked to the horizon where the sun had already risen, though it was still low in the sky. "Actually, no. I am realizing I should more often."

"You have been drinking," Wren stated, her tone more interested than judgmental. "My father used to like to imbibe every once in a while. He was so funny when tipsy."

"Where is he now?"

"He, my mother, and my older sister all died from the pox." She sighed but then chuckled softly. "Everyone in the household, except for Lily, my sister, were early risers."

"It must have been horrible for you, to lose your family," Grant stated. Although estranged from his father, he could not imagine losing him completely and finally.

Wren nodded and once again shifted the basket. "The worst time of my life. Sometimes I wished to have gone with them, to avoid the pain. But now, I accept what happened and know there is a reason I am still here."

"Perhaps to brighten my day," Grant said, without thinking. He scrambled to come up with something to add but came up blank.

"Why thank you, Mr. Murray," Wren said, then motioned toward the estate that came into view. "I think it is best you allow me to dismount here. I do not think Lady Roberts will take kindly to seeing us together."

The lass was quite astute.

"She can be very..." Grant started but wasn't sure how to finish.

"We are from different social standings. Based on that, it is best not to be seen together," Wren finished for him with the exact right words.

Grant dismounted, took the basket from her, and placed it on the ground. Then he wrapped his hands around Wren's small waist and lowered her to stand beside her purchases. Her legs gave a bit and she fell forward onto his chest.

For a moment, it was as if time stood still. Wide eyes and parted lips lifted to his face, and it took all his willpower not to kiss her. Instead, he chuckled and ensured she was steady.

Her cheeks pinkened prettily and she held out her arms. "The sway of the horse must have unsteadied me."

Lifting the basket, Grant held it out to her. "When do you have a free day?"

"Only Sunday. My aunt and I go to church." She shrugged. "Thank you."

"Can I call on you?" It was the stupidest thing he'd ever uttered. Grant wasn't sure what had come over him.

Wren must have thought the same because a frown marred her face. "What?"

"Perhaps we can go for a ride. Or you can visit me… at my house."

Her eyes moved from him to the side and then back to him. "What are ye expecting from me?"

"Nothing," Grant said, holding out both hands. "I enjoy your company, that is all." He took a breath.

Brushing her windblown hair from her eyes, she studied him for a moment. "I enjoy yours as well, sir, but you must understand that we can never be friends." After a moment she added, "Thank you so much for the ride. The walk would have been tiring." With that, she turned and walked away.

Grant remained rooted to the spot, unable to look away from the soft sway of her hips. He had not actually meant to ask to see her again. Had he? It would be utterly ridiculous.

The hangover was what had prompted him to suggest calling on her. She was but a maid, not that he thought it meant she was beneath him. It was just that there was absolutely nothing to be gained from any kind of assignation with Wren. His firm policy was that he only forged relationships with women who could help him financially, and as lovely as she was, Wren had nothing material to give him.

He mounted and continued to follow her progress until she went through the gates. It was only then that a thought occurred. What if she told someone? Rumors would fly between the servants, and no doubt reach Lucinda's ears quickly.

Turning the horse around, he raced down two streets until turning the corner and arriving back at Lucinda's townhouse. He went to the front door, and as he hesitated before knocking, the door opened. Lucinda stood in the doorway behind her personal maid. Apparently, she was about to leave.

There was disapproval in her gaze as it traveled over him. "Why are you here? Your appearance is dreadful." She stepped back from the door and shoved her maid forward. "Put my things in the carriage, I will be there shortly."

"I returned because I need to speak with you about your offer. To help me with the sponsorship of the ship. Lord Johnstone will inquire—that is the only reason I ask." Bile rose in his throat, and he struggled to clear it.

"You are to meet his lordship like that?" Lucinda's eyebrows rose. "Honestly, Grant, what has come over you? You have not been yourself lately."

"Of course, I am going to bathe and change before meeting him. And I promise you that on Saturday, you will find me without fault." He gave her what he knew was a devilish smile. "Allow me to see you again tonight."

Despite her obvious disapproval of his appearance, her lips curved into a smile. "If only. I have a prior engagement. The Astors are entertaining tonight. Unfortunately, my son has insisted on escorting me," she said, referring to one of the most prominent families in Glasgow.

Of course, her son would insist on going. It would be beneficial for him as the family had three daughters, one of whom was a current debutant and seeking a husband.

"I am disappointed." Grant met her gaze and pretended to have forgotten about the money. "I will see you soon, then." He took her hand and kissed it. "Enjoy your day."

He went to the doorway.

"The money will be in your account today," Lucinda called after him. "I do not like to see you so distracted. Make sure you are not seen in your current state by someone we know. Perhaps wear a cloak."

Since his back was to her, she could not see his triumphant expression. Taking the cloak proffered by the ever-proficient butler, he called out, "Thank you, my darling." When he glanced over his shoulder at Lucinda, he gave her what he knew was a seductive expression. "Enjoy your evening."

CHAPTER SIX

"PERFECT TIMING," COOK called out as Wren entered the kitchen, cheeks warmed by dashing through the gates and into the house. Still breathless, she only managed to nod. Her heartbeat had yet to slow after the encounter with Grant Murray. Now, she glanced around the kitchen wondering if any of the cook's assistants noticed her discomfort.

"There you are." Her aunt appeared in the doorway. "A word."

Her stomach plummeted. Had someone seen her with Lady Roberts' friend? They walked out to the side of the house and just past the garden gate. Her aunt scanned the surroundings.

"See that you remain away from Lady Roberts' sight. Do your best to stay away from the windows near the parlor and *never* walk past the kitchens."

Wren couldn't help looking at the area in the garden where she was to work. "Why? What will happen if she sees me? What has happened?"

Her aunt's lips pressed into a thin line, and she gave a slight roll of her eyes. "Despite her age, she wishes to be the most attractive woman in the household. I do not know if you have noticed that most of the servants here are quite plain."

"I had not," Wren replied. "But what does that have to do with anything?"

Despite the tone of the conversation, her aunt chuckled. "Lass, you're bonnier than most."

Wren waved her comment away. "Be that or not. I will avoid being seen and will wear my straw hat low on my brow."

"Good lass." Her aunt looked past her to the garden. "You do not have to work here. Perhaps Lars can get you a position in one of his shops in town. I hate to see you toiling outside." Her cousin Lars owned a printing shop in town.

But Wren didn't want to go to town. She liked working in the garden and being out of doors. "For now, I do not mind. Once winter comes, if they still wish me to be outside, I may have to reconsider."

Her aunt shrugged, probably realizing that she couldn't change Wren's mind. At least now. So they went back inside, and Wren ate before heading out to work in the garden.

Tim was surprisingly energetic that day. Wren wasn't sure why the change until she noticed that the maids had thrown open the windows on the second floor and were shaking out the linens. The maids peered down on occasion to ensure no one was directly below. Tim would wipe his brow with a flourish, and glance up to ensure they saw him.

Weeding was time-consuming, but it was also a thoughtless activity that gave her time to consider what to do about Grant Murray. The ride to the estate had been like no other experience. She'd ensured to keep the conversation light to keep from allowing herself to muse about the proximity of his body against hers.

The smell of whiskey on his breath made her wonder where exactly he'd been and from where he was coming. Twice she'd seen him in a state of disarray, which was unlike the time when he'd visited Lady Roberts and had been impeccable from head to toe.

No matter what his state, he remained too handsome for words, and she knew it would be a horrible mistake to allow any kind of friendship to continue between them. The repercussions could be very bad for her since, if Lady Roberts found out, she would not hesitate to fire her, or worse, also fire her aunt. Yes,

Wren could possibly find employment in town, but where would Aunt Mairid go? She was too old to seek new employment, and Wren wouldn't make enough money to support them both.

Still, she couldn't help but think about how he'd asked to call on her. *Strange.* Surely it was to toy with her, as there was no other plausible reason for his statement. Wren shook her head, recalling the skip of her heart and the plummeting of her stomach when he'd posed his question.

A phrase had immediately popped into her mind: "*Yes. Yes. I do wish to see you again.*"

From here on in, she'd do her best to avoid him. Wren looked up to the window, and realizing she was just outside the parlor, she quickly ducked. Not only was she to avoid windows, the front of the estate, being in rooms other than the kitchen, but now she also had to hide from Grant Murray. Still, she couldn't help herself from giggling at her situation and Tim gave her a questioning look.

She worked hard, and by the end of the day, Wren could barely stay awake. Exhaustion filled her entire body and she fell asleep on the ride back home. That evening, they ate a simple meal, after which Wren bathed to remove the dirt from her body and climbed into bed.

The next morning, she woke feeling refreshed and wandered into the kitchen. Her aunt looked up. "You look much better. Do not overdo it today."

Wren sat and ate the porridge, her aunt motioned to her and said, "I will spend most of the day bundling herbs, which means sitting on my bum."

"LADY ROBERTS EXPECTS company and wishes for you to fill these with flowers," Berta, the housekeeper, told Wren as she motioned for two lads to place four large vases on a side table in the kitchen. "I will tell you where they should go once you are done. There should be flowers in the garden, or about, I hope."

The vases were quite large, and she wasn't sure there were enough flowers in the garden to fill them. Not only that, but the woman had insisted that there be plenty of blooms for the upcoming event she was hosting.

"Where am I to get flowers?" she asked Cook.

The woman shook her head. "The Lady expects us to perform magic at times. I suggest you hurry and ask Rufus to take you to a shop in town."

Wren raced outside and to the areas surrounding the house, but Rufus was nowhere to be found. At her wit's end, she paused and scanned the area. There was a small corral where the household horses were allowed out to feed. She noticed there were wildflowers amongst the tall grasses along the edges of the fence. She hurried to the garden shed, grabbed shears, and went back.

Finally, she was able to make arrangements of wildflowers, tall grasses, and just two flowers from the garden in each vase. Wren embellished them with some cattails that grew wild in the swampy areas behind the shed. In the end, she was satisfied. Her head swam and her hands shook with exhaustion as she went and found Berta.

If the housekeeper found the arrangements lacking, she didn't give any indication. Instead, she was worried about hurrying to place them. "I will carry these two. Bring the other two."

Wren felt a wave of panic wash over her. "I do not think I should go in other areas of the house. My shoes are muddy and…"

"Take them off," Berta snapped. "Come along."

In stocking feet, she followed behind Berta, who carefully placed the first vase on a side table. The second one was placed just inside the front door.

Then with Wren holding the last two, they went to the sitting room. Once inside, Berta paused, placed both hands on her hips, and studied the room before turning to take one of the vases. She set it on a beautiful round table in the center of the room before she stood back and considered the effect.

If only the woman would hurry. Wren couldn't risk being seen by Lady Roberts. She stole a glance over her shoulder to the door. So far no one was about.

"I should have had you make five," Berta murmured. "Perhaps here is better." She picked up the same vase and went to a different table and placed it down. "Yes. That's better."

"Yes, that is a good place," Lady Roberts said from the doorway, making Wren jump.

She kept her gaze down and performed a slight bob. "My lady."

Berta looked at the woman. "Would you like the last on the center table or over by the window, my lady?"

The only sound was the clacking of the older woman's shoes as she crossed the room and studied the flower arrangement Berta had just placed down. "Interesting. I do not recall seeing *these* anywhere in the garden." She placed a hand under the wildflowers. The delicate purple flowers were quite common, but in Wren's opinion, they were also beautiful.

Then Lady Roberts moved to Wren. "Plant more of these." Before Wren could reply, she turned to Berta. "You decide where to place the last one. I need to ensure all is perfect and have no time for this." She walked toward the door and hesitated in front of Wren. "Who are you?"

Her stomach plummeted. She'd been in the woman's presence twice now—three if one counted her arrival—but it had only been from afar that the lady had seen her. Of course, someone like Lucinda Roberts took little notice of the servants.

She kept her gaze lowered and her face downturned. "I am Mairid's niece, my lady. My name is Wren. I work in the garden."

The woman slid a glance to Berta before turning her attention to Wren once again. "See that you do not work there today. I cannot abide someone mucking about outside my window when

44

I entertain."

"Of course… my lady," Wren said, the entire time wondering what her aunt would say. Not only had she not managed to hide from the woman, but she'd been spoken to by her.

"Berta, a word when you are done." With that, the woman swept from the room, leaving a trail of a rather strong floral perfume in her wake.

"No!" HER AUNT exclaimed, her face mottled with bright red spots. "What do you mean you picked wildflowers and *grass*? Child, what were you thinking? Why didn't you ask one of the footmen to take you to town for flowers? I am shocked Berta did not think of it."

"I should have asked." Wren lowered her head onto her folded arms on the table. "I am going to be dismissed, I just know it."

"Let us pray not." They sat in the large dining room just off the kitchen that was designated for the servants.

Wren let out a long sigh and met her aunt's gaze. "The arrangements turned out very pretty. Lady Roberts admired the flowers."

"That is good." Her aunt didn't seem convinced. "There is nothing to be done now. I must go oversee the last of the laundry. You stay out of sight. Go work in the garden shed."

Upon arriving at the garden shed, Wren opened the slender door and then pushed open a shutter. Inside, the mossy smell of grass and herbs helped settle her nerves. Hopefully, the "word" the lady of the house had to speak to Berta about had nothing to do with Wren.

It was late afternoon, almost evening, when a pair of carriages arrived. Wren couldn't help but to stand and peer out from the shed to watch as several women descended from the carriages.

They were all older, like Lady Roberts, and all were dressed in finery of every color. Most wore shades that were much too bright for women their age and far from flattering.

Moments later, several more carriages arrived. Again, the women who arrived were older. Intrigued, Wren watched the pageantry of colors, feathers, finery, and heard their chatter.

And then, a different kind of guest arrived. This time, men came to the house, some in carriages, a few on horseback. All of them were much younger than the women, though—much like those women—they too were dressed in fine suits in vibrant tones.

Wren climbed atop a bucket to see better, enthralled. She'd never seen so many handsome men, dressed in shades that one would not normally consider masculine.

Then a carriage arrived, and a familiar figure alighted. It was Grant Murray, wearing a beautiful outfit of deep purple. The shade flattered his dark hair and, with the suit tailored to accentuate his well-formed figure, he was a dashing sight.

As if sensing her perusal, he looked toward the garden. Although it was doubtful he could see past the hanging herbs, Wren shifted sideways out of sight, and when she peered out again, he'd walked toward the front of the house and had disappeared from her view.

Moments later, music wafted from the house, accompanied by loud laughter and singing.

While she tied herbs and hung them to dry, her feet tapped along with the lively music. She loved music, and had loved to dance at the village fetes growing up. It had been a long time since she'd heard music. And although the kind inside the house was nice, it was very different than anything she'd ever heard before.

"It is time for us to go home." Her aunt appeared at the shed entry. "The wagon awaits."

"I lost track of time," Wren admitted, standing to remove her apron. "I am enjoying the music whilst working."

Ever so slowly, her aunt turned toward the house, a deep, disapproving scowl on her face. "They will continue until late into the night."

"I am sure they are enjoying themselves," Wren replied, wondering why her aunt didn't seem to like the fact Lady Roberts entertained. "Do you not like music, Aunt Mairid?"

There was a visible shift, as her aunt tried but failed to smile. "I *do* enjoy it. Come, lass, the others are waiting." Even though she said she enjoyed music, however, she made one last scowl toward the house as she urged Wren forward and away.

CHAPTER SEVEN

T HE SMOKE FROM someone's cheroot made Grant sneeze and he stumbled forward, his drink sloshing out one side of his glass to dribble over the back of his hand.

Once again, he'd imbibed too much, which meant he could barely stand unassisted. Someone took his arm and instantly he stiffened as he recognized it was Lady Roberts.

"Grant, darling, Milly and I feel neglected." Lucinda pulled him to a settee where her friend sat, dress top pulled down, her sagging breasts spilling out and resting upon her abdomen. "We require you."

Lucinda shoved more than guided him down to the settee. She gave him a push so that he fell and sprawled across it and spilled the rest of his drink. The room spun. Before he could right himself, she quickly untied the front of his breeches, her lips curving as she reached in and grabbed his cock, pulling it free.

"We wish to play with you," Milly purred, her overly made-up face looming over him. "Be a good lad and open," she said and pressed the tip of one of her flaccid, sagging breasts across his lips.

This was the price he had to pay for Lucinda's large deposit into his account and a game he'd been part of for almost half a year. With her mouth taking in his cock and him suckling on the other woman's breast, he looked across the room at the other men who were also being coerced into performing different acts for the pleasure of what most considered society's highest class of women. In his mind, he was in a garden, a place far away. Instead of stale perfume and unwashed bodies, he was surrounded by fresh air and sunshine. Before him a woman stood, arms spread, face up to the sun. The women's moans dragged him back to the present and he pushed them away.

"I think I'm going to be sick." It wasn't a lie, his stomach churned at the scene before him. How had he managed to ignore the fact that the price of his self-worth was much higher than any amount deposited in his account?

The room spun, and he let out a groan, falling back onto the settee. Then everything went black.

IN A HAZE, Grant woke sprawled across the foot of a bed. Cracking his eyes open, the lightness of the room informed him it was late morning. He was fully naked, which meant someone had undressed him.

A leg brushed against his, and he lifted his head to find two other people in the bed with him. One of the other men slept on his back with Lucinda sleeping by his side, her arm possessively across his stomach.

Good. Perhaps her interest in him was waning. Noiselessly, he slid from the bed and searched for his clothes. But none of the items strewn about were his. He cursed under his breath. Although the memories were dull and hazy, he recalled someone undressing him in the sitting room. Once again, he glanced to the bed, wondering if it was possible to take a sheet to wrap around himself.

Finally, he settled for one of Lucinda's flimsy dressing gowns that he found strewn on the floor and wrapped it around his waist. Then he made his way out the door and down the hallway, hoping one of the maids had collected his clothing.

He dashed down the stairs into the small sitting room he last recalled seeing, and closed the door firmly behind him. The gown fell from his waist to the floor, but he didn't care. Once dressed, he'd leave for what he hoped to be the last time. There were many excuses he could make to Lucinda for the following weeks. There were several balls that he'd already committed to escorting someone else to, and besides, she was going to be attending some festivities with her son.

At the sound of a feminine gasp, Grant whirled around.

A wide-eyed Wren stood by the window, cut flowers scattered around her feet. Instead of covering her eyes, her gaze roamed over his nudity. Then, seeming to catch herself, she whirled to face the window.

"I—I was not aware anyone was here." Grant hurried to where his clothes had been neatly folded and placed over the back of a sofa. "I came to dress. I undressed...here...last night..." He ran out of things to say.

"I will leave you to it," Wren said, still facing the window. "I can return and finish later. When...when you are done."

"Wait," Grant said. He grabbed his shirt and held it in front of his sex. "I must apologize."

She looked over her shoulder at him. "Whatever for?"

What indeed? Something in him, however, screamed for him to ensure she didn't think less of him. Was she aware of what happened there the night before?

"For startling you."

"It was I that frightened you, I think." Wren giggled. The pretty woman never ceased to amaze him. "Enjoy the rest of your day, sir."

"You as well." He took in the sight of her. Dressed simply in a frock, sturdy shoes, and an unflattering straw hat, she still outshone all the women who'd been in the room the night before. How unfair that she was born into a lower class and had to work so hard for a living.

Wren bent to pick up the flowers at her feet and placed them beside a vase. Then without looking at him again, she hurried from the room.

LORD JOHNSTONE'S EYES twinkled in merriment, and he laughed when Grant told him what had occurred. "That you continue to be entertainment for those depraved women is astonishing. It serves you right. The poor girl must have been petrified at a bare man appearing in the room." He began to laugh again, and Grant gave him a look. The night before was a huge mistake. The entire time he'd ridden away, he prayed Wren was not informed of why he was there. Although if he were to be honest with himself, she would eventually know.

But if he were in Johnstone's place, he would also find humor in what occurred. As awkward as it had been being caught naked by Wren, the situation was also rather amusing.

Along with Henry, he and Miles Johnstone had met to discuss the sponsorship that very afternoon. The last of the four, Evan, was still gone on holiday.

Henry, who'd already had his fill of laughter, shook his head. "If she is a virgin, she will be petrified on her wedding night after seeing your ugly bits."

"I think her expectations will be dashed upon seeing someone who is not me," Grant rebutted. Then he sobered. "In actuality, I do feel bad for the lass. I should have looked about before entering so abruptly."

"At the ball tonight," Miles began, referring to the way he'd proceed later today. "I will begin my plan to seduce and conquer." He lifted the glass of amber liquid and Grant caught a whiff of the strong alcohol. Instead of making him want a drink, it made him slightly nauseous.

He sipped his water. His head was still heavy from the night before and apparently, his stomach still roiled.

"I will be there," he replied. "Which means I must go home and rest up." He shrugged. "As for me, I do not have to do much more than ensure just enough attention to my benefactresses."

Miles's lips curved. *"Benefactresses,* is that what you call them?"

Usually, such jibes didn't affect him, but for some reason his lordship's comment annoyed him this day. Instead of a verbal reply, he shrugged casually, despite the clenching of his gut.

Even as Grant made his way outside, his stomach felt hollow, as if hungry. He flattened his hand over the flat span. It could be that he missed the meal the night before and it was time to eat. He'd ask Norman for something to fill his belly once he arrived home. His mood turned as gloomy as the sky above.

ONCE IN HIS bedroom, Grant paced. Sleep had evaded him and instead, the unusual hollowness in his stomach had prodded him to get out of bed and do something. Even eating hadn't made the feeling go away.

Annoyed, he pushed open the window and the room lightened. The view outside the front of the grand home was nice, a treelined road leading up to it. Over the treetops, he could see the city. He imagined every street bustling with activity, people going here and there, horses and carriages competing for space on the roads, and the shops' bells over each door ringing as customers entered and left.

There were so many people about, and yet loneliness filled him. It was not the first time; since leaving home, Grant had often been lonely. Adrift, without a set direction or a firm foothold on what it was that he wanted more than anything in life. Other than riches, and those didn't appeal to him as greatly as they once had. Instead, it was something else, something which couldn't be purchased for any price.

A man on horseback appeared and rode to the front of the house. It was a messenger. Grant set his jaw. Hopefully, it would not be Lucinda sending a summons.

At the thought, Wren came to mind. The only way to see her was to go visit Lucinda. However, he did not wish to continue the assignation with the woman. Especially not if it meant continuing to participate in the sexual events for which she had such a penchant. His friends would probably be hard-pressed to believe that, more than anything, he wished for a simple relationship with someone who he could talk to, and spend hours with, doing absolutely nothing. Indeed, it was hard for him to believe, himself.

Still, such a thing was impossible, of course, considering he had very little money of his own. So while he didn't long for wealth as he once did, the fact remained that without it, he wouldn't be able to support himself. Or anyone else.

Absently, he looked to the table next to the bed where a book was splayed open, to what page he couldn't remember. It was a copy of a story he'd written and sent to a publisher in hopes that it would be well-received. It was a story of a man's quest to find the truth behind a stolen treasure and how he had come to realize that it never existed to begin with. Sliding his fingers over the crisp paper, he wondered if anyone had seen it as yet.

It had taken three years, but finally, the story of his heart had been written. Once he'd completed it, he'd been unable to write anything else.

"Sir." Norman stood at the open door. "A note from your mother."

Grant reached to grab the small envelope from the butler and ripped it open so he could read the neatly written words, relaxing at the content. His mother wished for him to visit, claiming he'd neglected her as of late. It was true. He'd not visited in quite a few weeks, and if he were honest, he too missed seeing his mother. His father as well, although his patriarch and he were not on speaking terms. No more than a greeting had passed between them in a pair of years.

"Tell the messenger his services are no longer required. I will go visit Mother as soon as I am dressed." After the butler nodded and left, Grant washed his face and freshened his clothes before heading downstairs and out the door.

Not quite an hour later, a young lad he didn't recognize took his horse as he arrived past the gates of his family home. The house was in the center of a long street where prominent, but not elite, families lived.

The people who lived there were those who worked for the wealthy and were well-compensated for it in turn. Judges, lawyers, and actuaries provided well for their families. His own father was an actuary, a trusted financial advisor for several titled men, who paid him quite well. Because of it, both Grant and his sister Felicity had never wanted for anything.

The door opened and the familiar, craggy face of Gerard, the butler, warmed when he spotted Grant. "You are finally here," he said with a mock-stern expression. "Your mother is in the sitting room."

At the doorway, he hesitated as memories of many evenings in the room flooded Grant's mind. He and his sister had taken lessons in this very room. He'd spent many an hour sprawled in a chair reading or working on whatever their tutor had assigned.

Now his mother sat with a book in one hand and tea beside her on the nearby table. She looked the picture of a lady, her gray-streaked brown hair pulled up into an elegant style, a string of pearls around her neck. When she looked up, she dropped the book and lifted her hands. "Grant! I am so glad to see you."

Upon reaching her, Grant took her hands and leaned over, kissing both her cheeks in turn. "Mother. You look lovely."

"You look a bit thin. You should eat more."

"I have neglected to eat since Felicity has not been home to remind me," he replied.

Before he could utter another word, his mother got out of her chair and went to the door to call out for Gerard to bring a meal to the dining room. She turned and gave him a triumphant look. "We just finished tea not that long ago. Your father left for an errand and should be back shortly."

He lowered himself into the closest chair. "What have you been doing?"

His mother joined him, sitting to pour tea and then milk into a cup for him. Then she reached for her own cup, lifting it to sip. "I hear you continue to keep company with that dreadful Lucinda Roberts."

Vying for time, he drank his tea. "And you with the gossips, Mrs. Middleton."

At his comment, his mother chuckled. "I do indeed. It is one of the ways I can know what happens in society, which is useful when one's son is a reputed rake."

"You wound me, Mother," he teased. "You will be glad to hear that I plan to cut all ties with the woman, I promise you." Grant couldn't help but wonder how much his mother knew about the goings on at Lucinda's gatherings. He shuddered to think she was aware of exactly what did.

But then Gerard announced that Grant's meal was ready for him and they made their way into the dining room. The table was set for one, but along with the meal, another tea setting with iced biscuits was there so his mother could join him.

As he ate, she continued chatting. "Are you to be at the Boutwell's ball tonight?"

"I am," he replied between bites. "I am escorting Lady Gardiner."

His mother's nose wrinkled. "Honestly, Grant, she is twice your age, if not more."

"She is fifty, so not quite," he replied and met her gaze. "I know you do not approve of my... associations, Mother."

"I most certainly do not. I wish for you to settle, and produce grandchildren for me, and to be happy." She covered his hand with hers. "Why do you resist?"

He was about to inform her that he *was* happy when the sound of a throat clearing from the door got their attention. They turned to look at Grant Albert Murray Sr., who cut a distinguished figure in a suit tailored perfectly for his tall, lean build.

The greying at his temples and round spectacles did not distract from the older man's attractiveness. Despite the instant dryness of his throat, Grant was proud of his father.

"Darling," the patriarch greeted his wife with warmth, and then his gaze moved to him. "Grant. Nice of you to visit your mother." His voice grew suddenly cold, and his greeting clipped.

"Father." He wanted to say more. To again have the easy-going rapport that he'd once enjoyed with his father. But now, they never seemed to get past pleasantries. "How are you?"

"Well." His father looked to his wife, dismissing him. "I am here but for a moment, to get a ledger. Do not wait for me for dinner. It will be a long visit with Lord Atterby."

After he walked out, his mother sighed. "I wish more than anything that you two would make up. This…whatever it is between you can be cleared up if only you would sit down and talk." She held up a hand. "And before you say anything, I have said the same thing to Bert. He is as stubborn as you are," she said, referring to his father as only she did.

Grant remained silent for a beat then nodded. "I will. Soon."

CHAPTER EIGHT

AUNT MAIRID'S EYES were round as saucers, her hand splayed atop her bosom. "You happened upon a *naked* man in the house?" She spoke slowly, as if measuring every word. "Where?"

As much delight as she took in storytelling, Wren wasn't particularly happy to tell this tale. However, as she was unsure if anyone had seen Grant Murray go into the sitting room and then seen her leave, it was best to keep her aunt informed of what exactly had occurred.

"In the small sitting room. He walked in bare as the day he was born." She shook her head. "Why his clothes were there, I do not understand."

Her aunt visibly swallowed. "What were you doing inside? I told you to avoid being in the house."

"Berta instructed me to go and see about the flowers from the day before. She said to ensure they were still well-watered. I was worried, as they are but simple wildflowers, so I moved the ones that were starting to wilt into the sitting room."

"And a naked man was there?"

"No, he walked in when I was placing them on the table by the window. Gave me quite a start. Actually, I think we were both startled." Wren couldn't help but smile as a picture of a very well-formed Grant Murray came to mind. She'd taken a good look, for which she was glad. Upon noting her aunt's scowl, she ensured she recaptured a serious expression. "I am sure no one saw what happened."

"Who was he? Did he say anything?"

"Mr. Grant Murray. He apologized. He dropped whatever it was he had wrapped around his waist."

If possible, her aunt's eyes grew rounder. "Dear Lord in heaven."

"Then I said not to worry, or something to the like, and left the room in a hurry." Wren tapped the tip of her finger to her chin. "After I picked up the flowers I had dropped."

"Wren…" her aunt started yet seemed to run out of words. "You are not going to work today. I will make the excuse that you are ill. Hopefully, no one saw what occurred."

"If you wish. I can clean the house and do a bit of gardening." She considered the minuscule garden outside and had an idea. "I will speak to our neighbors and ask that they allow me to plant the entire area. Two of them have left their plots in neglect."

"Do as you wish, Child." Her aunt's lips curved. "I must say, you keep life interesting."

IT TOOK BUT a pair of hours to clean the entire home as it was small, and her aunt had kept it tidy. Wren went downstairs and knocked on the neighbor's door, and an elderly woman opened it. Upon her asking about planting and sharing the crop, the woman was more than happy to allow her to do it. The neighbor next door was just as enthusiastic. The only one she didn't ask was the neighbor who kept her small bit of the garden plot fully planted.

With a plan in mind, Wren grabbed a basket and headed to the city's market. She'd find wilted and inedible items which she could, in turn, use to plant.

Despite the cloudy sky, the walk to the market was pleasant, and before long, Wren had managed to find more than enough items to start the garden. Most of the vendors charged very little or nothing at all for the overripened tomatoes, potatoes sprouting eyes, and peas with opening pods.

Excited at her luck, she stopped at a vendor and purchased a cup of hot cider.

"Wren?" A deep voice behind her spoke.

Cider splashed over the side of her mug when she turned to find Grant standing just a small distance away. In a riding suit with a matching hat, he was the picture of a true gentleman.

After what had occurred, the vision of him bereft of clothing formed and she blinked, pushing the thoughts away. "Good morning, sir." She bobbed a slight curtsy. "How nice to see you." Her eyes danced over him. Then she gulped down the cider, which was a bit too hot, and sputtered. "Oh dear, that burns."

He peered down at her with concern. "I should again apologize for what occurred. Did you burn your tongue?"

She frowned up at him, ignoring the question. "No need to apologize, sir. I know it was unintentional. Unless you dropped the wrap on purpose." When his eyes widened, Wren almost laughed. *The poor man.*

"Of course, I did not. I did not think anyone was there."

"My aunt insisted that I not work today. She is afraid someone in the household may be aware of what occurred." Wren looked over her shoulder. "Please do not tell anyone you saw me here."

"Our secret," he reassured and peered into her basket. "Allow me to buy you something more… er…eatable."

Wren couldn't help but giggle. "They are meant to be wilted. I am going to use them to start a vegetable garden."

"I see." He didn't seem to, but Wren knew someone of his stature didn't have to know about practical things like growing food.

They fell into an awkward silence for a short moment, and Wren considered what to say next. Nothing occurred to her, so she blurted, "I best go. Have a good day, sir." Once again, she bobbed a curtsy and began walking away without waiting for his response. She wondered if it was rude to do so, but it was too late.

"I can walk with you for a bit." He fell into step beside her.

"You must have things to do, sir," Wren whispered sharply.

"I am all done." He motioned to a tailor's shop. "I am to attend a ball tonight and require some items that will be delivered." The tall, well-dressed man walking with her brought many a confused look in their direction. Grant didn't seem to notice, but it made Wren quite aware of the difference between them. "Do you plan to spend the rest of your day gardening? What of other pursuits like, perhaps, reading?" he asked.

Many people of her background, especially women, did not know how to read. Thankfully, her parents had ensured she and her sister attended school. "I will garden and perhaps write a few letters. But I do enjoy reading if I have the time."

She wanted to ask what he would be doing until it was time for the ball but decided it wasn't her place.

"Ah, if you enjoy reading, then you must enter this shop with me." He took her arm and guided her through the door of a bookshop. Then, to her astonishment, he took the basket from her and placed it just inside the door. "Pick something you would like. I wish to make amends by getting you something nice."

When she stared at him as if he'd gone daft, he added. "To make up for the incident."

Despite it being the most peculiar of circumstances, Wren hurried to find a book. She didn't wish to linger and quickly picked out a novel that had a pretty bound cover. Grant took it from her and added it to several items he'd chosen, including a set of pencils, a journal, and what looked to be a bound stack of papers.

"Wrap it all up together," he instructed the shopkeeper.

Feeling at odds being in the shop with him, Wren was glad when they stepped outside and once again she held the basket.

Grant placed the bundle inside of it and gave her a crooked smile, uncertainty playing in his gaze. "Have a pleasant day with gardening and writing letters, Miss Owen." He touched the brim of his hat and walked away whistling.

"What a peculiar man," Wren murmured. She crossed the street, praying there had been no witness to what had occurred. Her aunt was going to kill her.

BY THE TIME her aunt was due to come home, Wren was a bundle of nerves. Once again, she'd stumbled upon Grant Murray, and this time in broad daylight, at the market, where staff from the household were often sent on errands.

The old cloth she kneeled on cushioned her knees as she finished turning over the soil in the raised garden beds, and Wren pushed her hands into the soft dirt. In a bucket next to her were the vegetables she'd prepared for planting. Usually, gardening relaxed her, but gauging by the tightness in her shoulders and neck, she was not in the least calmed. She blew out a breath and stood, catching sight of the wagon coming to a stop in front of their home.

The driver, who worked at Lady Roberts' stables waved, and she lifted a hand in acknowledgement.

Wren hurried to help her aunt down, taking a proffered sack first and then helping the older woman down. Once the wagon ambled away, she picked up her aunt's sack and went to where her aunt stood, admiring the raised garden boxes. "You did a lot of work today," her aunt said.

"Cleaned the house and heated your delicious leek and potato soup—without burning it," Wren answered, doing her best to keep her voice level. "Come inside, you must be exhausted," she added.

Unfortunately, her aunt was quite an astute woman and gave her a questioning look. "What did you plant?"

"Err...tomatoes...peas..." Wren said, the word "peas" coming out as more of a squeak. "Potatoes," she added, swallowing.

Instead of making her way inside, Mairid looked around the small area, stopping to glance at the only other garden that was replete with new plantings. "Where did you get these? Did you spend all your earnings?"

"No." Wren hurried to a bucket filled with water and began rinsing her hands. "As a matter of fact, I got almost everything free of charge. People are so generous, I have found one has to but ask."

"People?" Her aunt shook her head and headed to the door. "I need a strong cup of tea."

Unable to prolong the inevitable, Wren followed her aunt inside. Inside, the aroma of the simmering soup filled the air.

"It smells wonderful." Her aunt seemed to have forgotten the earlier conversation as she took a towel and lifted the pot's lid to sniff. "We should eat early today. I wish to get some mending done before bed."

Her aunt went to her bedroom to remove her coat and apron, and Wren went about setting the table.

"You did so much, my room is refreshed," her aunt exclaimed with a bright smile. "Thank you."

That her aunt was so grateful made her chest tighten. The woman had taken her in and given her a home when no one else was able. In Wren's opinion, it was impossible to ever repay the kindness. "There is no need to thank me, Aunt Mairid. No need at all."

The older woman settled at the table, smiling brightly when Wren placed a cup of steaming tea in front of her. "Where did you get all the items, darling girl?"

"Perhaps we should eat, and I will tell you all about it." Wren hurried to ladle the soup into a pair of bowls and carried them to the table. Then she lifted the pan from the stove and placed it on a cloth in the center of the table between them.

"There wasn't any word at the house regarding Mr. Murray skulking about bereft of clothing," her aunt informed her. "It is unbelievable that he made it down the stairs and into the sitting room without being spotted."

"It was quite early. The chambermaids were not making up the rooms yet," Wren stated. "Most of the staff were probably receiving their instructions for the day."

"True." Her aunt slid the bowl of soup closer. "My mouth is watering."

Wren grinned. "I haven't eaten since this morning. I too am quite hungry."

"Why are you avoiding my question about the garden?" her aunt said between spoonfuls. "Surely you did not take the vegetables."

It was shocking her aunt would think her a thief. Then again, she had been quite mischievous as a child.

"I did not steal them. I asked for them and people gave them to me. Vendors… at the market. I was just there for a bit."

"Oh, Wren, what if someone saw you?" Her aunt blew out an annoyed breath. "Did you approach vendors that Berta buys from? They could mention you were there."

"I do not think so." Wren's stomach tightened, and the soup lost some of its appeal. And yet she was much too hungry to lose her appetite completely. "I did run into someone, however."

Eyes closed, her aunt blew air out of her nose. "Who did you happen upon this time?"

"Mr. Murray," Wren said and hurried to add, "Funny thing, he was walking by and stopped to apologize again for what happened and…"

"And hopefully that was it. He went on his way," her aunt interrupted.

"Well." Her stomach sank.

"Wren?" Her aunt's eyes rounded, just like the day before. "What did you do?"

"I couldn't be rude when he offered to buy me a book. I surely did not expect him to purchase pencils and other things for me. I tried to stop him, but he said it was the least he could do." She cleared her throat. "He is quite nice, do you not agree?"

This time her aunt placed both elbows on the table, palms up, dropped her face into her hands, and closed her eyes. "Dear Father in Heaven."

Unsure if there was anything else she could do, Wren spooned soup into her mouth. It was delicious; she'd have to remember to plant dill and basil for future dishes.

"Wren!" her aunt exclaimed and Wren dropped her spoon. "What time were you there? Because Berta went to the market today. I pray she didn't happen upon you and Mr. Murray."

"It was early, not long after you left." Wren eyed the remnants in her bowl. "I looked around and didn't see anyone familiar."

There was a long silence as her aunt continued to eat, deep in thought. Wren reached for the ladle, but her aunt snatched it before she could get it.

"I should have not gone. But I didn't wish to waste a perfect day to get the garden started. I assure you, Aunt Mairid, I do not think anything will come of this. I promise to be more careful in the future."

When her aunt visibly relaxed, Wren let out a breath. She would definitely do her best to avoid the handsome Mr. Murray from then on.

IT WAS LATE at night when a knock at the front door startled them. Wren opened it to find a distraught Laurel. "My aunt. She is quite ill. I need help."

Aunt Mairid hurried to dress. "Go fetch the doctor, Wren. He lives across from the bakery that we always go to. Insist he comes at once. He has a carriage and can bring you with him to Martha's house. Be with care, it is late, and that area can be dangerous at night."

Laurel wrung her hands, seeming to be on the brink of tears.

"I didn't think about going to the doctor. All I could think was to come and get help, Mrs. Mairid. Thank you so much, Wren. I best hurry back to my aunt." She raced away into the darkness.

Going in the opposite direction of where Laurel and Aunt Mairid had gone, Wren walked briskly, keeping close to the buildings. The city was quite scary at night, Wren considered as she hurried down a narrow cobblestone street. When footsteps sounded behind her, she quickened her pace.

"Oy!" A male voice called; it was followed by laughter. "Where are you goin' in such a hurry, lass?"

Wren broke into a run, praying whoever it was didn't follow.

CHAPTER NINE

THEIR CARRIAGE JOINED the line of others in front of the Boutwell estate, and Grant glanced outside to see how much longer it would be before reaching the entrance. Meanwhile, the wealthy widow, Lady Melinda Gardiner, scrutinized him. Tall and willowy, she remained a beautiful woman and was well aware of it.

"I hear you were in attendance at Lucinda Roberts' last soiree." Her pale green gaze met his.

"I was." He'd made it a rule not to lie to his benefactresses. If anything, he was brutally honest to ensure they could not later state he'd taken advantage of them in any manner.

Her lips pursed. "Is it true? About the frivolity that occurs?"

"What you have heard is true," he replied lazily, not caring that he confirmed rumors. If the woman asked, it was because she already suspected or knew.

He met her gaze. "Why do you ask?"

"I am not sure to approve of your participation in such… distasteful things." She lifted her pert nose. "Do you not care about your reputation? Or not wish to be held in high regard?"

He almost laughed. Instead, he allowed himself only a soft smile. "I am a well-known rogue, my dear. My tarnished reputation did not keep you away. Honestly, I do not care about the regard of others."

Instead of a verbal reply, she arched a perfectly-shaped brow. "You should care. In this world, one's standing in society counts for much."

By the time they'd arrived at the entrance, Grant had lost any desire to go inside. Instead, he wished to be home reading, or even having a tooth extracted, instead of facing the myriad of false morality and judgement inside.

"Would it bother you greatly if I leave after escorting you inside?" he asked his companion who visibly tensed. "I will not be good company tonight. Besides, you may not wish to be seen with someone of my reputation tonight."

The woman's cold gaze raked over him. "You are not as important as you think you are. You have a handsome face and make for an attractive companion, but you are not much more than an accessory. Do not bother yourself with walking inside with me." Just as she was assisted out of her carriage, she turned to him one last time. "Never contact me again!" With that, she hurried into the ball.

Grant sat back against the cushion of the carriage feeling lighter than he had in a long time. He looked out to speak to the driver. "Take me to The Grant."

Maybe he'd find at least one of his friends there.

He peered out of the window and saw a woman dash around a corner, and spotted two men in pursuit of her. *Wren!* What was she doing out at night, alone? He immediately hit the roof of the carriage with his fist. When it came to a stop, he called up to the driver. "Follow them. The ones chasing after the woman."

The carriage jolted forward, and he clung to the squibs when he almost fell sideways. It didn't matter; he only wanted to catch up to the men and stop them. In moments, the carriage had pulled alongside the men, and Grant leaned out of the window. "Halt at once!" he called to them.

Unfortunately, the carriage driver mistook this for a command and stopped the carriage. Grant had no choice but to jump out and run after the men when they rounded the carriage and continued after Wren.

He gave chase, the carriage suddenly rumbling alongside.

"Sir, what are you doing?" the driver called down. "Do you know them?"

"Go up and collect the girl," he shouted, just as the two men stopped and turned to face him.

When Grant held his fists up and prepared to fight, they grinned.

"A dandy like you will not be much of a challenge," one said.

The other shrugged. "It will be fun, at least."

With a flurry of swings they advanced, and Grant was glad to note that neither was much of a fighter. Thankfully, he'd often trained with Miles, a fan of boxing. As a result, he was able to get a couple of good hits in. An uppercut to the first opponent brought a howl of pain as the man covered his nose, blood streaming down his chin. The other received a punch to his stomach, followed by a second to the side of his face.

When the second one doubled over, the first charged toward Grant. He jumped sideways, punching the man's side as he lost his balance.

A furious, high-pitched growl made him turn to the second man just as Wren appeared from behind him, holding a brick in both hands. She slammed it across the back of the man's head. Before Grant could catch his breath, he was hit from behind by the first man who'd fallen and obviously gotten back up.

"Sir," the driver called out breathlessly as he left the carriage and hurried to them. Then all went black.

⟫⟫⟫⟪⟪⟪

WREN WASN'T SURE what to do. She had to get the doctor to see about Laurel's aunt, and now she had a barely conscious man across from her in a carriage that didn't belong to her.

The driver hadn't seemed worried about Grant as he'd helped him into the carriage. "He will wake up with a headache, but he'll be fine," the man had told her.

They arrived at the doctor's house, and upon her knocking persistently for what seemed too long, the door had been opened by a slender man in rumpled clothing who patiently listened as she explained the need for him to go hurry to Martha's home.

"But before you do, can you take a moment to look at the man in the carriage? He was assailed when helping me fight off attackers." Wren motioned to the carriage.

The doctor climbed up into it with his medical bag in hand, and then emerged a few moments later. He instructed the driver as to how to care for Grant before turning to Wren. "Now, will you come with me to see about Mrs. Turner?"

Wren looked first toward the carriage and then to the doctor. She knew she shouldn't even entertain the thought of not going to Martha's, but still—Grant had gotten injured helping her. How could she not make sure he was all right? "I think I will go with him and get him settled, and then ask the driver to take me home." Decision made, she climbed back into the carriage.

Grant was conscious when she got in, though he seemed less than focused. He looked at her with a surprised expression. "Hello, Wren. I expected you would like to go home. I can instruct the driver to take you there."

"I will see you settled first," Wren stated without hesitation and sternly. "You saved me, and I must ensure you are going to recover fully. The doctor instructed that you be kept awake for a few hours to ensure your lucidity."

When he frowned and his bottom lip stuck out, he resembled a petulant child. "I assure you I am well. However, I will not argue that you don't accompany me home."

They arrived at the dark house, and she wondered if anyone was in.

"Is the house empty?" she asked the driver as they helped a now limping Grant to the door.

The driver shook his head. "Norman and Rosalie are home, they have probably gone to bed. Norman doesn't wait up for Mr. Murray."

The door was unlocked, so they went inside. Grant shrugged them off. "I am perfectly capable of making my way up to my bedchamber." He turned to Wren. "You really should not fret. I assure you I am..." His expression went blank, and he fell sideways to the floor.

"I wonder what the last word he was going to say was?" the driver said, bending to help Grant back up. With a lot of grunting and several pauses to catch their breath, both the driver, who finally introduced himself as Benjamin, and Wren managed to get Grant into his bedroom.

She went downstairs, following the driver's instructions to get a bowl of water and to boil more for tea. She hoped she didn't have trouble with the stove; she still hadn't learned how to heat water in all kitchens. This particular kitchen was large, not as big as Lady Roberts'. She found a kettle and filled it, then put it on the still-warm stove to heat. While the kettle started to boil, she opened the cupboard to look for the necessary herbs the doctor had prescribed. She was just reaching for a jar when a deep voice boomed behind her.

"Can I help you?"

She yelped and whirled around, holding up the jar and preparing to defend herself with it. Somehow. But she lowered it when she realized she'd been accosted by who was— unmistakably—Grant's butler. He had that carefully dressed, haughty manner that she'd learned to recognize from the butler at the Roberts estate.

The butler gave her a droll look. "Who are you, and what are you doing here?"

"I—I..." Wren lowered the jar. "I was being chased by some horrible men while on my way to fetch the doctor for a friend's aunt. Mr. Murray saved me, but one of the men hit him on the back of the head. So the doctor examined him as well, and then Benjamin—the driver—and I brought him home." She held up the jar, and then turned back to the cabinet. "The doctor said to give him tea made of..."

"I will take care of it," the butler replied. He moved through the kitchen with confidence, lifting the kettle and pouring some water into a ceramic bowl, then pulling out a short stack of cloths from a drawer. "Here. You can take the water and these cloths to bathe his head." He handed her the items and directed her to Grant's bedchamber.

As she went up the stairs, careful not to spill the water, she wondered if this was a common occurrence. Neither the driver nor the butler seemed at all troubled about Grant's state. Nor did they seem to find her presence there so late at night particularly odd.

Upon entering the bedchamber, she found Grant sitting in the bed with his back against the headboard and the blankets up to his waist. He wore a light nightshirt open at the neck. His eyes were squeezed shut, and there was a grimace on his face. When hearing her walk in, he opened his eyes and looked at her then at the bowl in her hands. "You don't have to look after me. I can do it myself. Or I can wake Norman," he said. "He's the butler."

"He is already up and is making something for your head-ache," she assured him.

His chest expanded with a large inhalation. "I instructed Benjamin to see you home. He awaits." Grant held out his hand, so she hurriedly put the bowl down on his night table and wrapped his fingers with hers. He smiled, despite the obvious pain he was in, she moved closer.

"I wish you a quick recovery. Thank you so much for ensuring my safety," she said.

"What were you doing out so late? Alone?" He searched her face.

"I went in search of a doctor. My aunt's friend is very sick. I should have knocked on the neighbor's door and asked that someone accompany me, but I did not wish to tarry too long," Wren replied, noting he'd pulled her closer.

"Wren. You must take better care. I fret that harm can come to you."

She couldn't help a soft chuckle. "My aunt says the same. I really seem to fall upon the most peculiar of circumstances. It is a good thing I am a fast runner. I have no doubt I would have made it to the doctor's house before those reprobates could catch me."

"It certainly seemed so." Grant's gaze moved to her lips. "May I kiss you?"

At the unexpected question, Wren gasped, and she was sure the bump on his head had affected the poor man. "I do not think so."

Still, she found she'd moved closer instead of away even as she told him "no".

Then, to her utter shock, she kissed him. It was but a soft kiss. A reassuring kiss. *Yes.* That was exactly it. She meant to set his mind at ease. So why was she now wrapping her arms around his neck? And, oh my, why was he kissing her harder, and his hands holding her sides as if she were a precious item?

"Sir." The butler's voice was like ice water when it fell over her and she gasped, fighting to catch her breath.

"I best go," Wren said, her face burning. "I should not have…"

"Wait." Grant took both her hands and then smiled up at her. "I will call on you."

"Why?" she couldn't help but ask. They couldn't be friends. They could barely be acquaintances. They were of different classes and kissing wasn't something they could indulge in, never mind anything else.

Before Grant could reply, the butler cleared his throat. "Miss, the carriage awaits."

"Oh yes. Thank you." Wren whirled around and raced out of the room, down the stairs, through the foyer and out the door to practically leap into the carriage. Her aunt was going to take to her bed if she found out. Somehow she would have to keep what occurred a secret. That was it. *Of course.*

There was absolutely no reason to tell her aunt anything other than she'd fetched the doctor and returned home to bed.

After all, she had to leave for work early the next day.

By the time she was deposited at her house, she felt more settled. Except, she'd replayed the kiss over and over. And relived the feel of Grant's lips against hers. Not only that, but his scent surrounded her, it was as if a part of him, just a whisper remained. Each time she inhaled, her eyes fell closed, and her lips curved. Tingles had traveled over her, it was as if he was familiar and so very much a part of her. She was imagining things. Yes, that was it. A silly girl's reaction to being kissed.

Thanking the driver, who waited for her to go inside, it was as if she floated over the ground.

Was Grant also thinking about the kiss? *No*. He'd probably kissed many a woman. Once he recovered, he would realize he had mistaken her for someone else and not call on her as he'd said. Despite how delighted her heart was at the moment, in the morning she'd have to face reality once again: Grant Murray was never to be hers. The kiss had been just that—a simple gesture of gratitude. It was to be the only kiss between them.

IN THE MORNING, Wren woke up with a smile and automatically touched her lips. After dressing, she entered the kitchen to find her aunt at the table as usual. Despite having obviously stayed up until a late hour, she seemed rested and alert. Her intelligent eyes swept over Wren.

"How did you get home last night?"

"What?" Wren fought for an explanation that did not include too many lies.

"This morning when I walked here from Martha's house, I realized that the doctor had come directly. He did not say to have brought you here. He clearly stated to have come directly after you came by."

Wren's blood ran cold. "I—I was brought home safely. Nothing to worry about, Aunt Mairid. I best fetch my shawl." She turned and hurried back to her room muttering, "No. No. No," the entire way.

Thankfully, before her aunt could question her further, the wagon arrived, and they had to rush out. Wren had no doubt that her aunt would question her again once they returned home later in the day, and she prayed to have a good story concocted by then.

THE DAY ONLY grew worse. Wren had just walked into the garden shed when Berta appeared. The stern woman's expression did not bode well.

"A word." The woman motioned for Wren to go further into the shed and then she followed her in before closing the door behind them. In the cramped space, there was barely enough room for both of them, which meant the woman's face was uncomfortably close when she glared at her.

"I saw you the other day, the day your aunt claimed you were unwell."

"I found myself feeling better and decided to start a garden. So I went to the square to the market."

The woman's eyes narrowed. "How do you know Mr. Murray?"

Wren wanted to throw up. Her stomach seized and she gulped, pushing back the bile. "Mr. Murray?"

"Do not toy with me! I saw the two of you and it looked to me as if you and he knew each other. I saw you speaking to him in a manner that seemed quite informal. Then you and he went into the bookstore."

Unable to formulate a response right away, Wren could only stare at the woman, wishing this were all a horrible dream. "He is a kind person. He recognized me from when I delivered a message to him from Lady Roberts. He followed me into the bookstore, and I had nothing to do with it. I assure you it was nothing more than that."

The woman's nostrils flared. "You should have declined the offer. Have you no sense of decorum?" She stopped Wren from answering, her palm held up. "It should not have happened, a servant and a gentleman speaking to one another as if friends. It is more than obvious your aunt has not taught you the correct way to behave."

"It will not happen again. I will ensure it." Wren did not wish to lose her position at the estate. The income helped so much, and she wasn't sure her aunt would be able to help her anymore. Tears welled up but she blinked them away. "Please, Miss Berta, do not dismiss me."

"Word will get to Lady Roberts sooner or later. It is best that today be your last day." The woman's gaze flickered over her and softened as she observed Wren's tears. "You are a beautiful young woman. I am not surprised that you have caught a gentleman's eye. But beware, Wren. Men like Mr. Murray do not wish for more than bed sport with someone of our ranking."

"My Aunt Mairid, she and I need for me to work. We need the money." Wren tried to change the woman's mind.

Berta nodded. "I am aware." She pulled a small envelope from her apron pocket. "But this can't be helped. You must leave here. Here are your wages and a good recommendation for your next employer."

The woman left the shed then, and Wren sank into the chair stored in a corner of the shed. Tears overflowed her eyes, and she covered her face. Her aunt was going to be so disappointed in her.

"I WORRIED THAT she would have seen you. At least she gave you a recommendation. That is something." Aunt Mairid held the envelope. "Wren, I think you are best suited to work in a shop and not in a household."

When she told her aunt about the dismissal, she had not been surprised. It seemed Berta had spoken to her already. Since they'd known each other for almost thirty years, they had a friendship of sorts.

Truly, if Wren was honest, she was glad not to have to work at the estate. Her aunt was right, she was not meant for domestic work. A busy shop, interacting with others who were of her same class, was more the type of work she could better perform. "I will do better, I promise," she told Mairid. They'd already eaten supper, so Wren began cleaning up. "I will wash up, Aunt Mairid. Tomorrow, I will go to Lars and ask for his help with a new position."

Mairid nodded and held her cup of tea to her lips. "Very well. And whatever you do, please try to avoid Mr. Murray. Nothing good can come from it. He will only break your heart."

Wren was glad to have her back turned to her aunt. She'd not told her about seeing him the night before and thankfully, her aunt had not brought it up.

Hopefully, his plans to come to see her had been spoken while he was dazed from his head injury. Besides, why would a gentleman like him wish to call on her? It made little sense. Berta was right, men like him could not possibly be interested in someone of her low stature. He played a game. That was all.

"You never told me," her aunt suddenly said, and Wren closed her eyes, begging God that the subject be something easy to reply to. "How did you get home last night?"

Lying was not an option, and it was better to face the issue and move forward. "I was chased by two ne'er-do-wells down the street."

Her aunt gasped and her hands clutched the cup more tightly.

"I was not afraid. Not horribly because I can run fast, but they were almost to me and the doctor's house was within sight, but still a bit of a way."

"Oh my," her aunt exclaimed. Wren frowned when her aunt put her cup down with a thump and covered her mouth with both hands, looking up at her. "Go on," she said, her words muffled.

Wren pressed her lips together, deciding how best to continue. "A carriage came by, and it was Mr. Murray."

Her aunt's head went backward, and her chin lifted; she stared at the ceiling as if in silent prayer for what could come next.

"He called off my pursuers and took me to the doctor's house." She left off the fight, the injury, and having gone to his home. And she most definitely left off the kiss. "His driver then brought me home."

Her aunt's eyes narrowed. "Wren. Please tell me that is it and you will not see him again."

Just then she caught sight of a rider approaching outside, and Wren's stomach pitched. Not only with butterflies from seeing the handsome rider but the accompanying panic from how her aunt would inevitably react, especially after her warnings not to see him again.

"I will water the plants outside after tossing this dishwater. Relax, Aunt, and enjoy your tea." She hurried out, doing her best to not slosh water over the brim of the large bowl and onto the floor.

Unfortunately, as she reached the door and wrenched it open, the movement caused the water to spill over the sides. In her hurry, she slipped on it and went flying, water spilling all over her. Wren cussed and got up on all fours facing the exterior.

She stared down at the toes of two shiny black riding boots. She didn't need to look up to know who stood in front of her. "Oh no."

"Mr. Murray," her aunt greeted him as he bent to haul Wren up to her feet. His gaze scanned over her.

"Are you hurt?" he asked, then looked to her aunt. "Mairid."

Wren stepped back and looked down at her dress; she was a soaking mess. Dirty dishwater plastered hair to the side of her face, and something slimy and cold hung over her forehead. She reached up to bat it off and discovered it was a potato peel that had flown into the dish when she'd worked at helping her aunt ready the tubers for dinner. *Oh no.* She was worse than a mess.

Without a word, she moved past Grant and went out to the small garden to fetch water from the well to rinse off. Her aunt would no doubt have things to say to him that she'd rather not be witness to. It was humiliating enough to be seen in such a state and now, her aunt would point out to him that he was not welcome.

It was a terrible ending to the most horrible day ever.

CHAPTER TEN

"WAIT A MOMENT please, sir," the older woman said as she threw cloths onto the floor to sop up the water. She then motioned for him to walk over them.

When she lowered to the floor and began mopping up, he reached for the cloth closest and dried the area by the door. If the woman found it shocking, she didn't comment. Probably because she was already flustered by Wren's fall and his appearance.

She took the cloth from his hands when she finished and put the wet cloths into a wooden bucket by the door. "Wren can take them and rinse them out," she said in a brisk tone.

The woman had a pleasant face; in it he could see a slight resemblance to Wren. She was slender and had graying temples and bright blue eyes that bored into his at the moment, but she was too polite to ask him anything right away. Instead, she said, "Please sit down. I do apologize for that. Wren was in a hurry to reach the door and slipped when the water sloshed over the sides of the bowl she carried."

When he sat, she moved the kettle over the burning fire in the small hearth. "Tea?"

"Please." In truth, he had worked himself into a state of what he would say or do upon arriving at the humble home, vacillating between thanking Wren for taking care of him the night before and leaving her alone, or remaining longer and asking her aunt if he could continue to call on her.

But he couldn't. It would be daft of him to even consider any kind of relationship with her. He planned to continue his current lifestyle, which he was sure would not, *absolutely not*, include the lovely Wren.

Of course, once the ship returned in six months or so, he would be wealthy, and only then could he even consider changing his lifestyle, and maybe at that time he could make Wren a part of his life.

Dear Lord, what was he thinking?

And now Wren had yet to return. He suspected she was embarrassed and too nervous to face him after their kiss the day before and now, her fall. "I wished to thank Wren for last night," he began.

Her aunt placed the cup of tea before him. He wrapped his fingers around the homely and probably expensive, sturdy mug. It felt right in his large hands, unlike the dainty and expensive things preferred by Lucinda and ladies like her. "I believe it is she who should thank you for saving her from those men."

"Yes, they were up to no good, that is true. But she did care for me after I was hurt in the scuffle with them. Even so far as to ensure I was well before leaving my side."

The woman looked to the door and then to him. "You seem to be fully recovered."

"Yes, thanks in part to Wren, and my butler of course. She told him what the doctor suggested to make for me before leaving."

The woman's face tightened. "Mr. Murray—"

"I am so sorry. I am so clumsy at times." Wren returned, breathless. Still wet, but somehow she'd managed to dry her hair and mop the water from her dress. She no longer wore an apron, which he guessed had caught the brunt of the spill.

"Mr. Murray came to thank you for your care of him last night. In his home," her aunt said in a clipped tone. "It seems whatever the butler made caused him to feel much better today."

"Ah," Wren looked to him, her blue gaze anxious. "I am glad you're well, now."

"I did promise to come and visit today," he prompted and then looked to Mairid. "I hope you do not mind that I pay a short visit. How is your friend?"

"Martha is recovering, thank you for asking, sir." Her aunt met his gaze. "Can I inquire as to what your interest is in my niece?"

He held both hands up. "I assure you I do not mean anything untoward. I find I like Wren. She is very intelligent."

"She is, but she is also very bonnie," her aunt said.

Wren made a sound, a soft groan. "Thank you for coming, Mr. Murray. You are kind." She remained standing by the door, and he could tell it was a silent plea that he leave.

He stood. "May I have a word in private?" he asked Wren, then looked at her aunt to show her he meant to be respectful. "Just for a moment?"

After a scant second, her aunt nodded.

He followed Wren outside. She peered over her shoulder at the window where he was sure her aunt was watching and then walked closer to the corner of the house where it would be harder to see them.

"I am sorry, did you not tell your aunt about last night?" he asked. The entire time his gaze was unable to move from her lips. The memory of the kiss from the night before was too vivid.

She shook her head. "I did, but I left out the part of going to your house. I thought it was best left unsaid."

"And then I come and speak too much."

"It is always best to have the truth out in the open. I can barely keep a secret, and sooner or later I would have said something." She gave him a soft smile. "Do not fret over it."

They stood awkwardly for a moment. "How are you today?" he asked.

She shrugged. "I'm fine." Her lips thinned. "I lost my job at Lady Roberts' home."

He couldn't help but feel this was his fault. Had Lucinda seen them together? Or heard about...well, there were several times they'd been together before the situation last night. No doubt her jealousy affected Wren's position. He wished he could help, but was unsure what he could do. "I'm sorry." He might try to get her job back for her, perhaps. "Why?"

She shrugged. "No good reason really. I am going to find work at a shop. My cousin, Lars, he works in town and has many connections."

He couldn't help but feel responsible. "There must be something I can do to help."

Her hands came up, palms facing him, and she shook her head. "No. It is best I do this myself."

"Can I call on you again?" Grant wasn't sure why he'd blurted out the words, but once they were spoken, he was glad. "To take you to the park. Or to tea?"

"You cannot be serious," she whispered. "What will people say? Think?" Her face softened. "You are very kind to me. However, I must decline your offer."

He met her gaze for a long moment. "Wee lass. I can't accept that you don't wish to see me again. But I will make every effort to see you." He leaned forward, kissed her lips, then turned and walked to his horse.

After he'd mounted and gathered his reins, he looked down at her; she stood stock still, her fingers even now pressed to her lips, and he was sure she wasn't as unaffected by him as she pretended to be. He smiled and urged his horse into a walk, but not before he said, "You look quite fetching in wet clothes, Wren."

GRANT WALKED INTO his parent's home and was surprised to find it empty. When he'd last visited, he'd promised his mother to stop by weekly to see her and they'd decided that Tuesday was to be their day.

"Where did Mother go?" he asked Gerard, who'd taken his

coat and hat and stood holding them.

"I believe to the shops, sir. She left an hour ago," the man replied and inclined his head. "Tea?"

Just in case she planned to only be gone for a short while. "Yes. I will wait for a bit." He went to the sitting room.

Outside, the garden beckoned. Bushes were replete with blooms. Along with roses, there were foxgloves, peonies, hollyhocks, and primroses. He walked out to find himself immediately surrounded by the chirps of birds sitting on the branches of a pair of silver birches he'd helped his father plant. It had been a gift for his mother. There was a birdbath surrounded by more roses, and across from it a set of benches over which the branches of the trees hung to provide shade.

He walked to a collection of colorful pots he'd not seen before. In each pot, a plant resembling a tree had been planted. The thin frail branches showed the plant was still young.

"They are Japanese maples, very recently brought to England. A client of mine gifted them to me." His father stood next to him looking at the trees. "Your mother is entirely pleased to be one of the first to have them."

"I am glad for her. She will unquestionably have a gathering or two just to show them off," Grant replied, imagining his mother's happy expression.

His father nodded. "That is why she is not here. We have guests coming tonight for dinner."

How he missed times like this when he and his father held discussions about things that were not important. A passing conversation about family, or people in their social circle. For years, they'd not done so, and he hated that as soon as this current conversation began, it would end.

"I best go and see about things before I have to prepare for the evening," his father said, his tone changing from warm to brusque. "I will let your mother know you stopped by."

"Father," he said before the patriarch could walk away. "How have you been? You look well."

His father's dark brown eyes met his for a moment before looking away. "I am well. You?"

Grant nodded, unable to form words past the lump that formed in his throat. Unable to let his father go, he swallowed. "I am sorry. For everything. What I did...You do know that?"

"Are you?" His father looked at him, his gaze sweeping over his pristine riding outfit and to the luxurious and very expensive boots he wore. The pride he'd felt in his appearance before leaving the house was immediately gone. Everything he wore had been purchased by women. Women he slept with and escorted here and there. He was a kept man. Nothing better.

"I am sorry," he managed. "If there was a way to go back and change what happened, I would."

His father reached out to touch one of the maple's leaves. "It cannot be undone, Grant. What you did—your actions affected not only this family's reputation but devastated a friendship of many years. Not to mention, it ruined a marriage."

"I did not mean for it to happen." Grant wanted to feel his father's embrace. The tightness in which he used to pull him into it and pat his back. To once again be the recipient of warm pride-filled looks.

"Well, it did." His father faced him squarely. "And yet you continue on the same path. You sleep with married women. Perhaps ruin more marriages. I have forgiven you, son, but I can never forget what you have done. Or agree on the path you've continued to choose."

"Please." Grant lifted both hands. "I am going to change. I am to partly sponsor in a ship that will, upon its return, make me wealthy. I will not have to rely on anyone but myself."

His father's expression was sad. "Do you really think it means you are to be a changed man? Do you not realize that you will forever be indebted to whomever gave you the money for this endeavor?"

To that question, Grant had no reply. Instead, he remained still and unable to move, his gaze fixed on his father's retreating form. Needing to throw something, hit something, he decided instead it was best to leave. This was not the right time for a visit.

Unfortunately, this was when his mother appeared at the door. Her expression was so bright and happy, it broke his heart. "Grant, darling. You look so very handsome today."

"And you are a vision," he replied, leaning over to kiss her cheeks when she approached. Immediately, she turned to the maples. "Did your father tell you about them?"

"He did."

She took his hand and pulled him to a small table with chairs. "Have tea while I tell you about my day." Then she turned to gesture at the maid in the doorway.

As she requested tea be prepared and brought out to them, he closed his eyes and took deep breaths, doing his best to calm his thundering heartbeat. But when he heard her sit in the chair beside him, he opened his eyes to give her a wide smile. "Tell me everything," Grant said.

She began talking about what she'd been doing, and then about the maples. He nodded and continued to smile, but he wasn't really listening. He was still thinking about his interaction with his father. He drank a cup of tea and took a couple of bites of food; only then did he feel he could leave without upsetting his mother's day.

And then what? How would he spend the rest of his day? He thought of Wren, and wondered how she was currently occupied. Maybe gardening in her little yard plot. He wished he could return to her home and find out, even though he was fairly sure her aunt would disapprove. Was she already seeking new employment in the village?

All of a sudden, he realized he might have an answer to Wren's problem that would be perfect. "Mother, do you need any help here in the garden? A friend of mine is a wonderful gardener, and she requires work. She was working for Lady Roberts but was recently discharged."

Her mother's face hardened. "That woman is wicked. Rarely

keeps anyone in employment for long. Tell your friend to come by. It is perfect timing. With Anna gone," she said, referring to his sister's maid, "We are short of help. Cook will welcome a set of helping hands."

Glad that at least something good had come from the visit, Grant walked out of his parents' home and onto the sunny street. A groom brought out his horse.

His father's words weighed heavily upon him so that he couldn't bring himself to mount. Instead, he led his horse away. He could use a walk, fresh air, and time to think. There had to be a way to make things right between him and his father.

Upon arriving at home, he walked in and went up the stairs to his suite of rooms. Once there, he paced, trying to figure out why he could not calm down. Then he realized: in every direction he saw clothing, decorative items, trinkets, and in every single item he'd brought into his rooms, he saw the face of a different woman. Everything had been purchased by someone for him. He'd earned nothing himself.

Then again, he had in a way done something with the women in order for them to be so generous. After all, he had money in the bank; although his account was not huge, it was enough to live on for a couple years. It had been lucrative. It just wasn't something in which he could feel pride, or a sense of satisfaction.

Grant went to the window and threw it open, then leaned out to take some deep breaths. The fresh green air helped him settle, but the view of the city in the distance was a stark reminder of his life, and how dependent he was on others.

He'd spoken the truth when telling his father there was nothing he wished more than to return to that fateful day and change everything...

THE BALL HAD been overcrowded and hot. Despite the discomfort, he and Henry had decided it was a perfect place to pick out women to seduce. Both of them needed money. Henry had been disinherited by his father and he, well, he was game for the sport of seduction anytime.

When he'd gone out to the balcony, a woman named Eleanor Dupree approached. She was attractive enough, although much older. She smiled prettily, fanned her flushed face, and through what seemed like benign and flirty chat, she'd invited him to her home the following night with promises of "a special gift".

Expecting nothing much from Eleanor, once the conversation ended, he'd returned to the ball and had enjoyed a delightful interlude with the young widow who often entertained in her home; they'd become lovers of sorts. It was a satisfactory situation. Neither of them wished to be tied to the other, but they shared enough of an attraction for a once-in-a-while liaison.

As he'd promised, he'd gone to meet with Eleanor the next day. The Dupree home was more of a mansion, stately and dripping with the feel of old money. He'd been whisked inside and hurried upstairs by a maid, who obviously kept her mistress's secrets. There, he'd entered the older woman's overly-decorated bedchamber.

For a moment, he'd felt a flush of distaste. He didn't belong there. She was a friend of his parents, and she was married besides.

He should have heeded that instinct to turn and leave. Instead, greed had propelled him forward and into the woman's bed. The sex had been rushed, Eleanor seeming desperate for his touch. When a man's voice sounded, it had taken Grant several moments for it to register. Someone had entered the room.

A butler perhaps, or a footman?

Eleanor's face paled, and her expression of satiated satisfaction switched to one of sheer terror; he instantly knew it was the voice of neither a butler nor a footman.

"R-Roosevelt," her voice had trembled. "I—I…" She pushed Grant away. He didn't need encouragement and rolled off the mattress to quickly begin reaching for his clothes and pulling them on.

Roosevelt Dupree was one of the most influential men in Glasgow. With millions to his name and a great conglomerate of enterprises, there was little he did not benefit from. His steely gaze was focused on his wife, and he'd barely turned his attention to Grant as he'd addressed him. "Get out." He'd gritted the words in a low and menacing tone. *"Now."*

Grant had scrambled out into the hallway still half-naked. Several servants had witnessed the entire debacle. He knew then that there would be more consequences to come.

The repercussions had been swift. Eleanor Dupree had been banished to the country estate, where she remained still, three years later. And Grant's father had been the one to suffer; he'd not only lost the Dupree account but several others that accounted for a large portion of the family income. It had taken an overwhelming amount of diplomacy from his father to retain his remaining clients and weeks—no, *months*—of work, of speaking to people and apologizing for Grant's actions.

The rumors had been rampant. Everywhere he turned, the gossips spoke of little else except how he'd not only ruined a marriage but had practically collapsed his own father's career.

Grant had avoided his father for days and hoped that if he said nothing it would all—somehow—go away and be forgotten. That his father would forgive him. But one day he'd been beckoned to the study.

The conversation that day was prominent in Grant's memory. Every word his father had uttered was concise and piercing. It was as if he sliced into his skin with a blade while speaking, and Grant welcomed the pain. He'd been careless, without thought.

"You have not only embarrassed this family, and almost ruined us with your actions, but I have lost every ounce of pride I had in you." His father's disappointment dripped from every word. And finally, he'd said, "Grant, I would prefer if you left this house. I can barely stand to look at you. In fact, I would like you to leave at once."

"I am sorry, Father," he'd uttered over and again, but it was a feeble apology even to his ears. It still was, even now…

"SIR, THERE IS someone here to see you." Norman broke into his revelry. "Lady Roberts."

A groan escaped Grant's throat. The woman had the worst timing. If ever he did not wish to see her, it was then. But if he wanted that money, he had no choice, no matter how much the thought soured his stomach. "Thank you, Norman," he said before making his way down the stairs. He had to hide his true feelings and assume what he hoped was a pleased expression, as he walked into the sitting room. But Lucinda wasn't seated; instead she stood, imperious and obviously displeased—though for what reason, he had no idea.

"To what do I owe this pleasure?" he asked as he moved across the room to kiss her cheek. As expected, the woman turned her head away, something she did whenever she wished to display her displeasure.

He held back his own feelings of disdain, but kept a pleasant smile screwed firmly in place. "Lucinda. Please. Sit," he said, motioning to a chair.

"I prefer to stand," Lucinda answered, looking past him to where Norman stood.

"Tea?" the butler inquired.

"No," Lucinda snapped. "Grant will serve me." She motioned to the long table along the wall that housed several decanters. "You know what I like." After pouring brandy, he handed her one, noting Lucinda's hand shook. She took a large swallow as if fortifying herself. Then she fixed him with a stare. "Is it true? That you walked about with one of my servants? Out in the open?"

Her lips curled into a sneer. "Tell me it was a mistake. That you did not fuck one of my maids."

With Herculean strength, he kept his face relaxed and without expression. "Since when are you interested in who I happen upon and walk with?" Grant acted as if it was a joke, nothing to worry about. Wren's aunt worked for the woman, and the last thing he wished was to affect her. "I did see the girl who'd brought me a message. At the market. We spoke of nothing of importance, and she went on her way."

"You left off that you went into a shop with her," Lucinda exclaimed. "Do not lie to me."

"We were both going into the shop. It was not planned," he lied, hating to demean what had been a delightful experience by sharing it with the hateful woman. Seeing Wren's pleased, shy expression when he'd gifted her the simple items was something he'd not forget. "Lucinda, did you really come all this way to chastise me about speaking to a servant? I was not aware I could not speak to whomever I wished. You worry overmuch."

The woman's eyes narrowed. "When I have an intuition about something, I take it seriously." She drank again, this time finishing the contents of her glass. "Have you spoken to Tom?"

The change of subject told him the issue was dropped—for now—but he knew the woman well enough to realize she'd be keeping an eye on him for the foreseeable future.

"I have not. I will go to The Grant this evening. Perhaps he will be there."

"Apologize," she said, handing him her empty glass. "I must go. I have an appointment with the dressmaker. I need you to escort me to a gathering tomorrow night." Lucinda drew near and raised her hand to cup his face. "Be a good lad now, and see me to the carriage."

Just as she climbed onto the carriage, Lucinda met his gaze. "The chit has been sent on her way and no longer works for me. If she is seen with you again, her aunt will be gone as well."

CHAPTER ELEVEN

T HE WARMTH OF the sun was welcome while Wren hung several items she'd washed on the line to dry. But then her stomach tightened at the sight of a black carriage appearing.

It was Grant's, she had no doubt about it. She looked at the windows of the neighbors, wondering if people would begin to ask questions about the constant visitors in fancy coaches. When it pulled to a stop, the door didn't open and upon closer inspection, she noticed no one was inside. The driver climbed down and walked to her.

"A message from Mr. Murray. There is a need for someone to help in the household. He has asked that I come for you and take you to his mother's home."

"His mother's?" Wren looked to her doorway. What would her aunt think? "Does she live alone?"

"No, she and her husband. Mr. Murray's parents."

"I see." She wiped her hands down her apron for no other reason than nerves. "I will leave my aunt a note and then go with you." Wren hurried inside. This could be good. It *would* be good. She found employment! Surely, her aunt would agree.

THE HOME WAS in a well-established neighborhood. Through the carriage window, Wren saw a woman in uniform pushing a pram and several other women who were obviously servants, performing the tasks of sweeping walkways or gardening.

When the carriage stopped, she didn't wait for the coachman, but opened the door herself and climbed down unassisted. The front of the home had a wide stairwell with four steps leading to a large wooden door. There was a covering over the door and topiaries on each side of it.

The driver stood next to the carriage. He told her that he'd been instructed to wait until after she'd spoken with Mrs. Murray, and then he'd been told to take her home.

So she climbed the stairs and knocked on the door. "Miss?" the butler said when he opened it.

"Yes. I am here to speak to Mrs. Murray. Her son, Grant...er, Mr. Murray—well, I just received word that she requested I come." Wren hated the trembling in her voice. For whatever reason, her knees became unstable as she was shown in and told to wait by the front door.

If the man thought it untoward that she came to the front door, there was no indication. Wren craned her neck to catch a glimpse of the interior of the room to the left. It was a sitting room. The house was much smaller than Lady Roberts', however, the décor was tasteful and made the home feel welcoming.

After taking a few deep breaths, she heard footsteps approach. An older woman, albeit much younger than Lady Roberts, appeared. Her gray-streaked hair was pulled up into a fashionable style which gave her a sophisticated appearance. Her afternoon gown was a pale green which suited her olive complexion perfectly. Upon meeting the woman's dark-brown gaze, Wren noted her eyes were just like Grant's. Not that she should notice such a thing, she reminded herself and bobbed a curtsy. "Ma'am. I am Wren Owen. Mr. Murray sent word that you would see me regarding employment."

"Ah yes, of course." Mrs. Murray's smile was friendly. "I am Grant's mother." She motioned down the hallway. "Come."

Wren followed the elegant woman, but she couldn't help peering about at the décor and details of the house. This was where Grant—Mr. Murray, she reminded herself—had grown up.

When they arrived in the kitchen, she saw a woman sat at the table drinking tea. The short woman stood, her questioning gaze on Wren. "Ma'am, you could have rung," she said, looking from her to Grant's mother.

"Mae, this is Wren. She is a...er, friend of Grant's. In need of work, I am told." Mrs. Grant looked to her for confirmation.

"I am. Yes," Wren acknowledged. "Very much."

Like her employer, Mae seemed kind, not worried about whether or not the lady of the house would admonish her for continuing to sit down when they'd walked in. So unlike the servants at Lady Roberts' home who were on edge whenever the woman was about.

"Please sit,' Mrs. Murray motioned to a chair, sitting down as well. Once Wren sat, the woman continued, "Now tell us what you did at Lady Roberts' home."

Wren produced the recommendation she'd gotten from Berta. "I gardened mostly. Cleaned floors and windows. I can do anything but cook." She frowned at her admission, then added, "I can sew, clean, wash..."

Mrs. Murray did not read the letter Wren handed her. Instead, she looked at the cook. "Mae does require help. We recently lost two of the help. One went with my daughter, and the other married and moved to live with her husband."

Mae shrugged. "If the lad recommends you, that is all I need."

"Can you start tomorrow?" Mrs. Murray asked.

When Wren nodded, she was told how much she'd make, which was almost twice what she had been paid at Lady Roberts' home. Of course, her duties were to be double, as she'd serve as a chambermaid, cook's helper, and clean the downstairs.

"We have a room and would prefer you live here," Mae informed her.

"That's fine," she told Mrs. Murray. Though, she was surprised. Wren had not considered having to live there. Of course, it would be easier than having to travel every day. However, she would miss her aunt, and surely her aunt would miss her as well.

"I live with my aunt now, in the village. She's widowed, you see, and…"

"Of course. I understand. You can have Sundays off to visit your aunt."

Nonetheless, the offer was too good to refuse, and she accepted it without hesitation.

LAUREL WAS WALKING past when Wren was deposited back at home. She crossed the street and hurried to Wren. "Where have you been?"

"To Gordon Street. I was offered work there. At a house. Unfortunately, I have to live there now." Wren hated that she'd not get to know Laurel better. "How is your aunt faring?"

They walked near the garden. Laurel pulled her to a bench. "Your aunt will be sad that you will be gone most days. I work near Gordon Street, at the antiquities gift shop. You can visit me whenever you need to go and fetch items from the butcher or chemist."

Wren smiled. "The pay is more."

"I am glad for you." Laurel turned her face up to the setting sun. "Since Aunt Martha is better, I can return to work now."

They discussed how Laurel went to work and decided they'd hire a caddy the next morning to ride to town together, as it was too far to walk from the village.

"Here comes your Aunt Mairid now," Laurel said, waving when the older woman appeared. It occurred to Wren that she seemed more tired than usual lately. Probably from the added time of traveling after long work hours managing the laundry at the house.

Her aunt sat next to them without a word and let out a long breath. "It is a beautiful day, is it not?" she said, and like Laurel, lifted her face to the sun. "I do yearn for a long day to sit in the sun and do nothing more than allow it to warm my old bones."

"You should consider not working," Wren said. "I have a new position that will pay well. Between Lars and I, you will not want for anything."

Her aunt studied her for a moment. "Just a few more months and I will do just that. I am saving to ensure I am not a burden on anyone."

There were questions in her aunt's gaze, but she refrained from asking. Instead, she turned to her friend. "Laurel, how is Martha?"

MAIRID SAT BACK and took several deep breaths. Despite the fact that Grant Murray did not live with his parents and that it would be improbable that Lady Roberts would find out about it, something about the situation of Wren's new position did not bode well.

The man was much too interested in her naïve niece, and he was bringing her closer to him with each passing day. There weren't many options for women of their class if a man dishonored them. Worse would be if something were to happen and Wren became with child; she'd be without work and there would be another mouth to feed.

"You must promise me," Mairid began, making sure to get Wren's attention by taking her by the wrist. "That you will not allow Mr. Murray any liberties. He is interested in you and can take advantage of you working for his mother as leverage. Please make sure you let him know you will not stand for any disrespect."

Wren's cheeks colored and she blinked. "Do not worry, Aunt

Mairid. Although I am certain he is a gentleman, I promise you that nothing untoward will happen."

She relaxed. But only a bit. Wren was a delicate thing. Slight and lovely, reminding one of a forest Fae. Everything about her was beautiful, from her heart-shaped face to her large, heavily lashed eyes, and her cascades of auburn hair. Even her voice was musical, her country lilt giving it a singsong sound.

Upon her arrival, Mairid had known it would be but a matter of time before the lass would catch someone's eye, be courted, and then marry. However, Grant Murray's interest was not what she wished for the girl. Someone like him, of an established family in Glasgow, would never marry a servant girl. She prayed Wren would prove to be intelligent and see through the façade of interest to realize it was nothing more than a passing fancy for the man.

Sadness enveloped her. If her sister and husband had not died, Wren would have remained safe, protected by her parents from something like this. It didn't help that her own husband had passed recently, leaving such a large void, and making it necessary that she continued to work. Staying away from the house that held so many reminders of the past helped with her grief.

Everywhere there were reminders of her departed husband. At the same time, she wanted those reminders there. Things like his pipe on the side table next to his favorite chair; the smell of the tobacco was growing weaker every day. Or his scuffed boots that remained on the floor next to the wardrobe. And other things that Mairid couldn't bring herself to dispose of, even though she knew he'd never return to use or need any of the items left behind. She couldn't help but cling to any part of him, her wonderful Harry, that she could keep with her. One day she'd join him, but for now, her duty was to remain and care for Wren, who'd also suffered a great loss.

"You are worrying," Wren said, placing a hand over hers. "I do not wish for you to fret. I promise all will be well." At her smile, Mairid couldn't help the tightness in her chest. Still, the smile was so much like her sister's that in the end, it made her smile in return.

"Of course, I fret. You are what I have left of my dear sister. A beautiful reminder of her."

Wren blinked rapidly, her eyes welling with tears. "I miss her so."

"I know, dear. I do as well."

They enjoyed dinner and a cup of tea while discussing the week ahead. Mairid made Wren promise to send word during the week to assure her all was well. They decided that on Sunday, they would work in the garden together and make time to visit Laurel and Martha.

By the time Mairid lay down for the night, she was at ease. First thing in the morning, she'd send a message with a lad to Lars asking that he do something for her. He would be closer to the Murray house and he could check on Wren.

CHAPTER TWELVE

"I SUPPOSE IT is my turn now to come up with my funds," Lord Miles Johnstone said in a bored tone. "The timing could not be worse."

Evan, Henry, and Grant gave the peer time to continue, each with a whiskey in hand as they relaxed in the comfort of Evan's parlor. Grant's sister and brother-in-law had just returned from their holiday, and the group had immediately convened to discuss the rapidly upcoming deadline for the sponsorship.

"In two weeks, I must meet with Captain MacFarland and pay for the sponsorship," Evan stated. "I do request at least two of you come with me. I do not like the idea of carrying so much money to the shipyards."

Henry stretched and crossed his legs at the ankle. "You should send word and meet elsewhere. It is too risky. Each day we hear of different crimes committed at the shipyards. Men dressed like us are certain to attract attention."

"Very true," Grant added. "Perhaps his home would be better."

"I will send a message a day or two prior to the deadline. In the meantime, bring the capital here. I will place it into the safe."

They turned to Miles, who'd yet to utter a word. Instead, he swirled the amber liquid in his glass and watched it until it settled. "The woman I planned to seduce has found a lover and seems quite enamored. I must find another."

In spite of his words, no one was concerned about Miles, who had more than doubled his fortune since taking the helm over the family's accounts. The man was a genius when it came to finances. It was only because he enjoyed making wagers that he even cared to come up with a sum to obtain. All the men knew that it was a pittance for him and easily available even without needing a woman to seduce.

"I am sure it will be too easy a task for you, whether you have a week or a day," Grant said, studying his friend. "You seem glum. Or should I say, glummer than usual. Is something amiss?"

Miles' gaze lifted slowly to his. "Duties that must be performed on a regular basis. Attending this social gathering, a dance, or even the dreadful picnics by the loch, is tiring. I wish for nothing more than to go away to the country and not see people for an entire season."

If his family had such an estate, Grant would be a hermit, rarely leaving the country for the busyness of city life.

"What stops you?" Henry asked, leaning forward in his chair. "From leaving for a bit?"

"My sister's debut," Miles stated with a frown. "I can't very well allow her outing into society to be without someone to look out for her best interests." He held out his glass for a refill and Grant poured more whiskey into it. Then he continued, "Father would settle her with the first man who has a title and with no regard for the man's financial status. Meanwhile, Mother yearns for a sop who will fall at Penelope's feet and profess his love."

Evan studied Miles. "Attending all the required events works in your favor. It gives you ample opportunities to find the woman from whom you will reap monetary rewards."

"True," Miles replied. "There is the slight problem of how to acquire the funds without there being rumors that my family is ruined. It is a tightrope I must walk."

As their conversation continued, Evan wrote a note that would be delivered to the ship's captain; once it was completed, they settled down to play a game of rummy.

However, Grant's mind was not on the game and several

times, he had to refocus just to keep up. He couldn't shake the sickening feeling in the pit of his stomach of how he'd acquired the funds. Just as his father had warned him, he could feel an ever-growing and lingering cloud of shame and disgust over his head. He knew it would be there until he repaid Lucinda for every single cent.

Never before had his lifestyle bothered him in the least. Other than the seduction that had caused a rift with his father, which was the one tryst he'd always regretted, every one since had been an arrangement of sorts. And he'd been honest with the women.

Even Lucinda. He had spoken about the venture, and had informed her he did not have the amount required to invest. She had, of her own free will, gifted him the money. Perhaps his distaste lay in the fact that he disliked the woman and did not plan to attend any more of her vile *soirees*—if one could call them that. Nor did he plan to sleep with her again.

He shook his head, garnering the attention of his companions. "I am confused," he began and then said to them aloud what he'd been thinking, and admitted his feelings regarding how he'd gained the funds.

The men put the cards aside. Each one ponders his words. That they did not chide, jest, or belittle the admission assured him that they were undeniably true friends.

"I do believe our man is maturing," Henry said with a smile. Despite the man being younger than him by a pair of years, and only recently turned from his carefree life of leisure, Henry was indeed a changed man. Instead of spending his days avoiding his duties to the family estate and holdings, he was now an equal partner with his father, proving to be quite talented at financial dealings.

Evan spoke next. "You should return the money. Nothing is worth the cost of a burdened mind. Between the four of us, we can lend you the money."

Miles choked on his drink. "Thank you for volunteering me." He coughed again and Grant pounded him on the back.

"You have more money than Midas. You know you can afford it," Henry teased. "Besides. I agree with Evan. Grant should return the money to that horrid woman."

"You slept with her, and attended her gatherings. In my opinion, you are owed double the amount you'd requested from her, just for that," Miles replied with an uptick of his chin. "I suggest you just pay her back upon the ship's return as planned."

The conversation continued, each man detailing why Grant deserved the money. Although he expected that they would help him if he returned the money, he wondered if perhaps it was best that he follow the original plan, and wait as Miles suggested.

His thoughts went to Wren. Her humble life and honest way of earning a living made her much more honorable than he'd ever be. She was happy and fulfilled, without the burden of self-loathing that he carried. In that moment he envied her. He was afforded the best of everything, a grand home, tailored clothing, servants, and he had a bank account, and yet, none of it had he acquired by his own honest labor. Everything had been given to him due to his appearance, his attention and favors spent on vain women who used him for their own gratification. And he'd allowed it to happen, and even encouraged it.

Standing abruptly, he walked to the windows and stared unseeingly out into the darkness. The lack of light was reminiscent of how he felt inside at that moment.

It was only when he spent time with Wren that he felt lighter. The innocent, unselfish delight she took in simple things like the flowers of the garden or the journal he'd gifted her made him happier than he'd been in years. He wanted to do more for her, to spend more time with her.

"I know that look." Miles stood a few yards away, his gaze missing nothing. "It belongs to a man in love."

Grant's breath caught. "No. Of course not."

He neared to study Grant more intently, his right eyebrow lifting. "Who is she?"

"She's... There's no one." Was he in love? Even if he was, did he wish to admit it yet, to these men? They would laugh, perhaps, or worse, try to talk him out of the feelings Wren inspired. They were too dear to share, something he wished to consider in private. He turned away. "I bid you all good night. I must see to something early tomorrow morning."

CHAPTER THIRTEEN

A FTER TEA AND a tour of the house with Mae, Wren was left to begin her tasks for the day. The list of responsibilities was long, but Mae helped her to break the tasks into sections so that she could have a schedule of which rooms to see to, and when.

She learned that the man of the house often worked in his study and preferred not to be bothered. If he required any kind of repast, he would ask for it. The mistress spent most of her day in the sitting room or at social outings.

Mae informed Wren that Grant's mother enjoyed gardening and would often spend hours outside tending to the beautiful flowers. A gardener did come to the house twice a week for the heavier tasks of weeding and trimming, however, Mrs. Murray preferred to do most of the tending herself.

In the sitting room, the remnants of tea, cups, cakes, and cheese remained on a table and Wren went about clearing the dishes. Once she took them to the kitchen, she returned to the tasks of sweeping, tending the fireplace, and dusting.

Outside the glass doors, she caught sight of Grant's mother. Wearing a wide-brimmed hat, she kneeled on a pad and trimmed a flowering bush. Wren couldn't stop herself. She pushed open the doors, allowing the light breeze to carry the floral scents into the room.

Her employer turned and smiled. "Grant tells me you are an avid gardener yourself, Wren."

"Yes, ma'am, I love gardening. I keep a tiny allotment at my aunt's home, but it is only for vegetables."

She neared and peered at the bush the woman was trimming. The phlox was a brilliant fuchsia, the clusters of blooms a wonderful addition to any arrangement. Wren took a couple steps closer. "With it being mid-spring, you will have blooms for another month." She couldn't keep the awe from her voice. "It is rare for them to bloom so early."

Grant's mother sat back on her heels. "The walls help; there is no bitter wind to distract them from blooming. It's a bit cooler today, so I am cutting them back to force more blooms."

Just as Wren was to tell her that was a grand idea, her employer's gaze widened, and her lips curved. "Grant, darling, I am so glad you are here."

Something in Wren's stomach fluttered. She ensured a calm expression upon turning to greet him. As their gazes clashed, she realized she was holding her breath, and she released it audibly. If his mother noticed, she didn't show it. Instead, she accepted her son's assistance to stand and held her face up for him to kiss.

"The garden looks good. Is Wren helping?" he asked, his gaze never leaving Wren's.

Wren shook her head. "I merely came outside to admire the garden. By the beauty of it, Mrs. Murray does not require any assistance in gardening in the least."

The older woman's cheeks pinkened prettily. "I am not so sure about that. I do enjoy being outside with my hands in the ground. Please excuse me, son, I won't be but a moment. I must wash up." Removing her hat, she walked inside, leaving Wren alone with Grant.

"I will fetch tea," Wren said, turning away. Before she could take a step, he took her arm.

"I came to speak to you."

The low tone made Wren wonder if something was amiss. She whirled to face him. "What happened?" The slight curve to the corners of his mouth relieved her somewhat.

"I wish to know how you are faring."

"Oh." Wren looked to the doorway, and gently, but firmly, she pulled her arm from his grasp. Then she took a pair of steps to ensure proper distance between them. If either Mae or Grant's mother caught them talking, she could lose her position. "All is well. More than well. I could never thank you enough for helping me. I am indebted to you." She turned to leave. "If you will excuse me now, sir."

"Can I not visit with you?"

His question made her hesitate. Had her aunt been right in suspecting that his motives were less than honorable? What would happen if she turned him down? After one last look at the doorway, she turned to face him. "Sir, what do you expect in exchange for..."

"No, God no." Grant's eyes grew round, and he held out his hands palms up. "I do not mean to make you uncomfortable. If I ask to spend time with you, it is because I enjoy your company. Nothing more, I promise."

She leaned closer to whisper. "You kissed me."

This time he frowned. "Yes. True. Well. That was because I think you are beautiful. It was quite forward. Accept my apologies."

"Whatever are you apologizing for?" His mother reappeared, standing behind Wren. If only the earth could open up and swallow her whole, she'd be forever grateful.

"I..." Grant started.

"He does not owe me an apology, ma'am. I am indebted to you for this opportunity," Wren said. "I will fetch tea." She rounded her employer, not stopping until she'd gone through the parlor and stood in the hallway. She hoped further questions on behalf of Grant's mother did not lead to her dismissal.

When she returned with a laden tray that Mae had assured Wren she'd filled with Grant's favorite bites, both mother and son seemed in good spirits. They'd moved to a table in the garden. It was shaded by a tree, making it perfect for teatime outdoors.

As Wren poured tea, Mrs. Roberts seemed to study her but

said nothing.

Grant, on the other hand, seemed to think it was the perfect time to have a conversation. "Have you begun to use the journal?"

What would his mother think? She kept her eyes on her task and hoped the heat in her cheeks didn't appear too apparent. "Yes, sir. I appreciate it very much."

"And the pencils?"

"They are perfect." She put the teapot down and stepped back.

"What of—"

His mother cleared her throat, her keen gaze moving from Wren to her son. There was a slight tightening around her mouth. "Grant, if you purchased the items for the lass, you should allow her to use them when she can. When it comes to journals and such, one must take one's time."

Although the woman's comment was delivered in a light tone, Wren didn't feel reassured.

"I am glad," Grant replied, then continued, "I will fetch you on Sunday morning and take you home. I have business to do in that area."

"There is no need, sir." The beating of her heart was so hard, she could barely breathe.

"On a Sunday?" his mother gave him a questioning look. "What kind of business?"

Grant let out an audible breath. "It is not hard work, just speaking with someone."

"Is there anything else you require, Mrs. Murray?"

His mother shook her head but said nothing, so Wren hurried back into the house.

Once in the kitchen, she paced from one end to the other. Thankfully, Mae was not there. In all probability, she was having a rest before she needed to make dinner preparations.

Wren went to the window to peer out at the garden. Grant and his mother were having an animated conversation, and she had a sinking feeling that it was about her. She knew his mother would never approve of their friendship, and although she was new to working in a household, she was sure a friendship between a man of his class and hers was most unheard of.

Why did Grant push things? Was it because he wanted to garner his mother's attention, or because he liked to toy with others' emotions? No matter what he said or did, Wren could not believe he was at all interested in a friendship with her. She had nothing to offer someone as highly educated and worldly—or wealthy—as him.

Footsteps sounded behind her, and Wren turned from the window. Mae entered and smiled at her. "I needed to rest in my room for a bit, but then I realized I am quite hungry. Have you eaten?" The woman went to the cupboard and rummaged for something to eat, bringing out a bit of ham and a half a loaf of bread, and some cheese. As she began cutting the bread, she looked over her shoulder at Wren. "Sit, Child. Let's chat."

Wren lowered herself onto a chair. She did need to discuss something, and right now Mae was the only person she knew at the Murrays. She hoped what she had to talk about wasn't going to cause her problems, but the cook seemed like a kindly woman who would probably have good advice, much like Aunt Mariad. "I actually could use your advice. It's about a...delicate situation."

Mae brought the slices of bread, and the cheese and ham to the table on a cutting board.

She sat and continued to slice the food for them to prepare into sandwiches. "I see. What is it about?"

Wren took a deep breath. "It is about Mr. Murray. Not the elder Mr. Murray but the son, Grant."

"He was such a delight when a bairn. Grown up to be a proper gentleman, he has." Mae hesitated. "There is the matter of his roguish ways." The woman shook her head. "Tell me what it is, lass."

"I brought the tea to him, and Mrs. Murray. He informed me in front of her that he would fetch me on Sunday and take me home." Wren covered her cheeks as they heated up again. "I declined the offer. Why would he say all that in front of his mother?"

"Oh." Mae's expression resembled Mrs. Murray's, with a slight tightness around her mouth. "What kind of friendship is there between the two of you?"

"I-I have only seen him a few times. He has been kind since I met him. Do you not find it alarming that he would seek out a simple woman like me?"

Mae chuckled. "You are quite bonnie. So there is that. It could be he is attracted to you. Still, Child. Do not allow him any liberties. Men need limits, especially those who are used to women flocking to them." She moved a few pieces of bread, some cheese, and ham onto a small plate and placed it in front of Wren.

"You wound me, dear Mae," Grant said as he strolled in. He did not look wounded in the least.

The woman lifted her gaze to study Grant with a pensive expression. "I hear you planned to fetch the lass on Sunday," she said to Wren's mortification.

"It is too far for her to walk," he replied to Mae with a grin. Then he focused on Wren. "Can I have a moment of your time?"

Wren looked to Mae, who motioned to the doorway with a silent expression, very clearly indicating she should tread carefully.

"Very well," Wren said.

They walked out of the kitchen to the back door that led to where the stables were. Once outside, Grant frowned down at her. "You seem perturbed at me."

He was so impossibly tall and broad-shouldered that Wren had to lift her chin to peer up at him. She took a step back to make it easier to meet his gaze. "It is that, well... I am surprised that you would so casually state taking me home to your mother. She cannot possibly approve of a friendship between us."

"I am an adult male who does not require his mother's approval as to who I am friends with. I told her we were friends when I asked that she consider hiring you. It is not like it is a surprise to her." His statement did not help her feel better.

Unable to stand still, she walked in a circle and came to stand in front of him again. "And I am a woman. No matter the difference in our stations, we are opposites in many ways. A friendship between us is most unconventional. And unacceptable. You must know that!"

Before she could take another turn, he grasped her elbow. The touch was startling, not only because it was unexpected, but because her body immediately reacted to it. Wren stood silent, waiting to hear what he'd say.

"What if I am interested in more than friendship?" His voice deepened. "What if I wish to court you, Wren?"

"What?" She swallowed as her mouth and throat went dry. "Me?"

"Yes," Grant said with an earnest expression that bordered on uncertainty. "I think about you constantly. I find it impossible to go an entire day without seeing you. Whenever I consider the future, I picture you in it."

"I am not sure what to say." This was most extraordinary, so very unexpected. Her mind had gone blank. Grant had most certainly lost his wits, and once he recovered would take the declaration back.

The only thought that finally permeated was how very handsome he was, and how horribly it would hurt when he realized this mistake when the words he'd misspoken in haste would be taken back with an apology and she'd have to pretend all was well.

"Can you tell me what you will think about it? What I've asked?" He'd yet to release her arm and Wren felt as if she could not move. To move away would hurt him, but to remain made it impossible not to reach out to him. Grant took the decision from her, by releasing her elbow. It was as if a void filled her until he cupped her chin and lifted her face to him. She could only search his eyes, surely the truth of how he felt had to be there.

"You are so beautiful. A rare jewel," Grant said, and then he took her mouth with his.

Her eyes closed and she fell against him, giving into the kiss, wanting more from him. Desire like she'd never known surged through her.

Grant's lips moved over hers in a way that was so very intimate. When his tongue sought permission to go past her lips, she parted them. This was most definitely much more than a kiss. The ground shifted, and she grasped his shoulders to keep from falling.

When his arms encircled her and she was flush against his hard body, what had been embers of desire exploded into flames. From the top of her head to the tips of her toes, every part of her body tingled with untethered heat.

Wren tugged him closer, sure she'd die if he ever stopped kissing her. When he moaned against her lips, she wanted to cry out with happiness. How was it possible to feel so alive from a kiss?

"Wren." Upon hearing her name, Wren realized Grant had broken the kiss and was holding her.

Her eyelids fluttered open, and she gazed up at him. "What happened?"

"You were overcome with…er… passion."

"Did I faint?"

"No, you simply kept your eyes closed for a long moment."

"Oh." Wren pushed him back and swayed on her feet. When he made to move closer and ensure she was stable, Wren held her arms out. "No… don't touch me. I may become overcome again."

Grant laughed and she frowned at him. "You are a dangerous man. My lack of control is not comical, but quite disturbing. You cannot ever do that again."

"Will you still consider my courtship?" Once again, uncertainty crossed his features. "I am quite sincere in my declaration."

It was as if she'd come to from a wonderful dream, and her mind remained hazy. First, she took inventory of her legs to ensure she could walk without falling over, and then she touched her lips, which she was certain were swollen from his kisses. Lastly, she ran her hands down her apron.

All the while, Grant studied her with interest, seeming confused. Thankfully he didn't question her and instead waited patiently for her to finish without speaking.

Certain all was in order, and that she could walk and more importantly not run straight to him to beg for more kisses, Wren cleared her throat. "We can speak on Sunday. I am afraid I cannot keep a single thought in my head at the moment." With that, she rounded him and ran into the house. Once inside, she turned from the kitchen to her small bedroom.

Whatever had come over her to allow what happened? She'd just promised not only her aunt but also Mae had warned her not to allow him liberties. Not only had she allowed him more than a fair share of liberties, but she'd taken plenty of her own. Had she really touched his back, his shoulders, and his face?

A giggle escaped her and Wren pressed her lips together. Grant played a dangerous game. She was sure he toyed with her. Although, he had seemed quite genuine in his request of courting her.

She sat on the bed. Who could she possibly discuss the turn of events with? More than anything, she needed advice from a neutral party.

Wren stood and walked to the basin where she poured cold water and then took a cloth and dipped it into the water which she pressed against her lips. There was enough time to walk to the shop where Laurel worked and return before it was time to help with dinner. Once satisfied that her lips were not swollen, she went out and to the kitchen.

Mae barely glanced up from the dough she kneaded.

"Can I nick out to the shop two blocks down for a moment?" Wren asked.

"You can do better and stop at the butcher to pick up the meat I ordered. They were supposed to deliver this morning and have yet to. Get some sausage for the morning while you're there." Mae motioned to a basket on the table. "Money is in the basket. Make haste."

Wren collected the money and picked up the shopping basket by the door. She hung it by the handle over her arm as she went outside. The day was cloudy, with rain-threatening, but Wren didn't mind. Anytime she was outdoors it was freeing. As the butcher shop came into view, she crossed the cobblestoned street and entered. From behind the counter, the butcher waited for her to approach.

"I am from the Murray's home. Mae sent me to pick up to-day's order, as it was not delivered this morning."

The man was visibly upset at the mistake, adding an additional cut of meat for the household. Then he'd weighed some sausage, wrapping it in brown paper as she waited. As he worked, a slight man emerged from the back room. He looked from her to the butcher with questioning eyes.

"You forgot to deliver to the Murray's," the butcher bit out. "Second time this week you forget something."

The slight man's eyes rounded, his face turned blotchy, and Wren wondered if he was about to cry. "I delivered all morning. Went by the list," he said in a clipped tone.

The butcher didn't acknowledge him. After a moment, the slight man shrugged and returned to the backroom.

"I apologize, miss. Please tell Miss Mae, I am sorry." The butcher handed the neatly wrapped parcels over the counter to her and she put them into the basket.

From there it was but a few yards to the small gift shop where Laurel worked. A bell dinged overhead as she walked into the cluttered shop. There were shelves of different sizes on the walls, every single one filled with different items. Tables were set here and there, not seeming to be in any sort of pattern. Howev-er, the items atop them were organized by function. Some had bells, another had perfume bottles, and still another was laden with candlesticks.

Laurel appeared from the back of the shop and her face brightened at seeing her. The young woman rushed to her. "Wren! I am so glad you came by." They hugged and smiled at one another with glee.

"I may just have to volunteer to pick up from the butcher, on occasion, so I can see you," Wren informed her.

When an older man peeked out from a side door, Laurel motioned to Wren. "This is my friend, Wren, she stopped by for a quick visit."

The man nodded. "Tea?"

"Thank you, no," Wren said. "I cannot tarry."

When the man disappeared, Laurel motioned to a pair of chairs near the window. "This is where I take my tea. That way I can look outside and watch people walking by. I saw Lars the other day. He said he went by to visit your aunt."

"Good," Wren said, placing the basket on the floor next to her feet. "I have something to ask you. You will not believe what happened today."

At once Laurel leaned forward. "Tell me."

When Wren finished telling her friend about the kiss, albeit an edited version she could not bring herself to speak of all the sensations, or of how long they'd kissed. Or of his tongue inside her mouth for that matter. She then told her of Grant's question.

"He asked to court you?" Laurel covered her cheeks. "Oh my."

"Do you think he is sincere?" Wren asked. "I find it hard to believe."

"I do as well." Laurel bit her bottom lip. "You did say he announced his plans to fetch you on Sunday in front of his mother. That was very odd."

"I agree. She was not pleased." Wren glanced out the window as an elegant couple walked by. It occurred to her she didn't own one thing that would be appropriate if ever she were to accompany Grant anywhere.

A woman stood at the window to study a vase that was prominently displayed.

Laurel smiled. "I am quite proud of my display. The vase and open book garner a lot of attention." A frown crossed her features when she spoke next. "If I am to be honest, will you be cross with me?"

"I won't. I promise." Wren waited for what she knew would be a confirmation of what she already knew.

"Do not go forward with any kind of assignation with Grant Murray. He is known for his roguish ways. I cannot see how it would end well for you. I would hate for you to end up with a broken heart. Or worse."

It was too late, her heart was already shattering. Since he'd asked, Wren already knew the answer she would give. It was best to get it over with, to let him know she would not allow such an inappropriate relationship.

She sighed and nodded. "You are right, of course. It is exactly what I thought. I will come here on Sunday, early, so we can go home together. It is not appropriate for me to ride alone with a gentleman."

CHAPTER FOURTEEN

"A WORD," TOM Roberts said in a clipped tone.

It was late on Saturday and the hotel lobby was crowded. Grant had just decided to leave; he'd grown bored, and his friends had long gone home. Being a bachelor was lonely. The revelation had come to him after Henry and Evan left to their wives.

Miles had gone to London on business, which left him alone. Except for the son of his lover.

Grant motioned to the chair facing his and waited for the man to lower into it. He'd never cared for Tom Roberts. Not only because he was an elitist, but also because the man spent most nights in dens of inequity, yet had the audacity to look down his nose at others. Obviously, Tom had garnered his dark tastes from his mother.

Then again, who was Grant to judge, as he too had participated several times at Lucinda's gatherings and with the goal of more than pleasure.

Tom was short with a round face that had yet to garner the look of maturity even though he had to be in his thirties. With sallow skin from lack of time outdoors and wild curls that resisted any kind of control, he seemed sickly. However, from his bright gaze, it was obvious he remained very alert. "Mother tells me you rarely darken her doorway as of late. I am glad to hear it."

Since the man asked no question, and Grant preferred not to speak to him about his relationship with his mother, he remained silent and waited for whatever else Tom had to say.

Tom continued, "You must have found other women to sleep with in exchange for money? That is what whores do, is it not?"

The insult stung, but he allowed it to slide off his back since it was spoken by someone engaged in similar, dark pursuits. He nodded. "Indeed. I find that I do not need to entertain her as much."

"Eventually your looks will fade, and women will stop using your services." Tom's lips twisted into a sneer. "A sad ending indeed."

"Do you know why these types of women will always need someone like me?" Grant asked, leaning closer.

Tom's eyes narrowed, but he didn't reply.

"Because they are desperate for attention. Their husbands ignore them, and their family the same. Sons and daughters never visit other than when forced, as they eagerly await their mothers' deaths and, by turn, the inheritance."

The man's face turned to stone. "Because you fuck for payment, does not mean you know anything of what happens within the families."

Grant smiled because he knew how to anger the man further. "Being I have spent more time with your mother in the last months than you have in years, I would beg to differ."

"Stay away from my family," Tom bit out a bit too loudly as several men turned in their direction.

"Have a good evening," Grant said and stood.

Before he could make it to the door, Tom came up behind him. "I mean it. Stay away from my mother."

There was something akin to fear in Tom's narrowed gaze. Grant wondered if there was something afoot. He let out a breath. "If it isn't me, it will be another man. The person you should be demanding change from is your mother."

Tom shoved him as he passed and hurried outside. All composure gone, he rushed to a waiting carriage and climbed in.

For a few moments, Grant stood out on the road wondering what exactly happened and if he should go see Lucinda. No matter that the woman was somewhat depraved, he had spent a lot of time with her, and there was no doubt that the woman was growing older, and weaker. Her gatherings would not last much longer and she'd find herself alone. A sad ending indeed.

Again, he was reminded that his own bachelor's life wasn't much different than Lucinda's. Both of them were alone.

"MR. MURRAY," THE butler at Lucinda's house opened the door wider and waited to take his hat and overcoat. Grant handed the items to the butler. "Will you please let Lady Roberts know I am here?"

"Of course, sir." The butler walked away in the strange way that butlers had of moving both unhurriedly and quite rapidly at the same time. He stood, waiting, feeling unease even though the sitting room was familiar. A faint smell, a mixture of men's and women's perfumes, hung in the air. Apparently, Lucinda had recently entertained.

Just as he lowered to a seat, a maid walked in with a tray. Upon it were a teapot, two cups, and tea cakes. She set the tray down on the table nearest his chair. "Lady Roberts will be down momentarily." The servant poured tea into one cup for him and then quietly left.

It was long before Lucinda walked into the room in her usually overbright gown and perfectly coifed hair. "Darling!" He stood and moved to her. A slight purpling under her eyes informed him of her lack of sleep and he could only imagine what she'd been doing until the early morning hours. As it was now late afternoon, her guests had been roused from wherever they'd slept, or better yet laid in before being sent on their way after being served strong tea, bacon, and bread.

"What brings you to see me today?" Lucinda said, accepting his kisses on her cheeks.

"Can I not come and see about you? Ensure you fare well?" Grant asked, waiting for her to sit. Once she did, he followed suit and poured tea for her. "How are you?"

The woman ignored the tea and pressed a hand upon her breast. "I am charmed that you visited. I had hoped you'd come last night. The affair was extraordinary." Her voice trailed off. "You did not deem it important enough for even a reply."

Grant took her other hand. "I do apologize. I would have not been good company." He'd seen the invitation and had tossed it into the fire.

"I am planning to travel again," Lucinda informed him. "For an extended amount of time. Perhaps two or three months." She fixed him with what he knew she felt was an inviting expression, but it failed to entice him. "Come with me."

He held up his hand. "Lucinda, before you continue, I want you to know. I saw your son, he is very much opposed to me having anything to do with you. In fact, he demanded in no uncertain terms that I am to stay away. I prefer not to cause a rift between you." He paused. "Besides, I find myself quite busy with my book."

"Book?" Lucinda looked at him as if he'd lost his mind. "I am speaking of a month on the continent, extravagant parties, unmatched experiences, and yet you'd rather work on a damned *book*?"

"I'm concerned about what Tom said…" Grant began but trailed off. Why was Tom taking a sudden interest in his mother's affairs? He'd never taken much notice or care of her before.

Lucinda waved a hand dismissively. "My son finds himself in a bit of trouble. I refused to help him, this time. He squanders so much money on unseemly pursuits, and I don't see why I should pay for it. He had enough money in his accounts that the interest alone should have given him substantial income."

So the man was in debt. *Interesting.*

Even more interesting was her description of her son's activities. Grant itched to ask what Lucinda considered unseemly. After all, the woman hosted orgies in her home.

But instead, he nodded as if he understood.

"I will speak to Tom," Lucinda added. "Our actuary will have to deal with those matters." Then she shrugged as if the entire matter with her son was not important. "Now, about what I asked. Will you come on the trip with me? I would love to repeat the wonderful experience of the last time we traveled together." She pursed her lips and leaned forward.

Grant pretended not to notice that she aimed for his mouth and pulled her into a tight hug. Then, he released her and sat back. "I cannot promise to go with you. I will see about some things and will let you know." He stood. "I must go. I have a matter that has to be dealt with."

Lucinda did not let him leave so easily. "I expect a reply in the next day or so. Whatever issues you have can be dealt with swiftly, I am sure."

It had been a bad idea to visit her. She'd be relentless until he gave her an answer. If he said no, she'd sulk and expect him to make some sort of recompense for not going with her.

She continued speaking, following him to the door. When the butler brought him his coat and hat, she clung to his arm, and he could see sadness and possibly fear in her eyes. It was sad in a way. The woman had had every opportunity for a good life. She was extremely wealthy and had the world at her fingertips. What she didn't have was love, and he knew better than anyone—that couldn't be bought. Still, after the butler had moved to a discreet distance, he leaned closer and said into her ear, "Have you considered marrying, Lucinda? You are a beautiful woman and deserve someone who is dedicated only to you."

He meant it. The woman was desperately lonely and no matter how often he or anyone escorted her to events or attended her soirees, as time passed she would be more and more alone. As she grew older, Lucinda would not be able to continue her current lifestyle.

"I would lose control of my money," she snapped. "I could never allow someone to have that hold over me." She looked out to the scene before them at her manicured front lawn with its ornate iron gates under a just as ornate arch. "I will not." With that, she turned and walked back up the stairs.

Riding away from Lucinda's, Grant considered what would happen to the woman. He knew there were many ways she could keep her money away from a husband. But that required someone she trusted. From her reply, it was obvious she didn't trust anyone. It was sad really, but not his concern.

He didn't want to end up like Lucinda. Alone. Wren came to mind and his heart eased at the thought of her. Still, there was another matter he needed to resolve before anything else. It was the most difficult situation he had, and he needed to repair it; as doubtful as it was that the issue could be resolved, he would dedicate all his energy to it. His life depended on it.

GRANT ENTERED HIS parent's home and went directly to his father's study. If his sire was surprised to see him, the man's expression did not divulge it. Instead, he motioned to a chair. As he sat, Grant mused that the study was much like it had been most of his life. Side by side, ledgers lined shelves in a filing order only his father understood. More of the books were stacked, balanced precariously atop one another on the edges of his large oak desk. Centered on the desk, opened, was what looked to be a new ledger with neat lines of numbers and notes halfway down the page.

"What is it, Grant?" His father probably expected that he'd ask for money, or for some other kind of support.

"I wish to have a discussion with you, Father. When do you have time?" Grant's heart thudded in his chest, reminding him of when, as a child, he'd been called into the room because of a transgression. It took several breaths to calm his pulse and even then, his chest tightened. "Please."

For a moment his father frowned as if perplexed by his request. It was, after all, the first time he'd come with such a request. There was apprehension in his father's tone as he pushed the ledger aside and replied, "I have time right now."

His father stood and rounded the desk, then he peered out into the hallway. At seeing someone, he asked that tea be brought and then he returned to his seat.

"It is much too early for something stronger, and I require a clear head to continue with this." He motioned to the open ledger before looking up at Grant. "What is it?" The brown gaze was unwavering at meeting Grant's. Such strength his father possessed. He could only pray to be as strong one day.

"I wish to apologize again for the troubles I brought upon the family and the effects of my actions on your work," Grant began.

A crinkle formed between his father's brows. "You have apologized before, Grant, but I find it hard to believe you are sorry when you continue to live the life you lead."

"I am cutting ties with the women," he answered. "I will be self-sufficient once the ship that we've sponsored returns."

His father nodded. "I am glad to hear it. However, the only reason you have the funding for that ship is because you are Lucinda Roberts' lover."

The gasp at the door caught their attention. Grant turned to see Wren in the doorway holding a tray with the items for their tea, stock still, her eyes wide. His father motioned for her to enter. "I did not mean to shock you, lass. I should have closed the door." He smiled at Wren. "We will serve ourselves."

His stomach sank at how she'd visibly paled. Once again, his actions caused someone he cared for hurt and anguish. Without looking at Grant, she hurried out.

His father motioned to the door. "Close the door, for goodness sakes. The lass looked about to faint. Not often we see such innocence."

There was nothing to be done about Wren at the moment. Once he finished, he would seek her out and explain. How he would explain it, he wasn't sure. He closed the door with a quiet click, then turned back to his father. "I will ensure Lucinda gets every cent back," Grant said. "You are correct, she did gift me the funds because we were lovers. However, I am determined to put that lifestyle behind me." Grant poured the tea, his gaze moving to the decanter on the side table, wishing he could drink something stronger. But perhaps it was time to put that behind him as well.

His father watched him pour the tea and reached for his cup. "I hope so. It is time for you to consider marriage and a family. Society's memory is very long. You may find it difficult for a family of good standing to approve of you as a match for their daughter. Not impossible, of course, but it will not be easy for sure."

Grant nodded and sat back in his chair. "What about us, Father? Where do we stand?"

His father stood and went to the window. "What you did was careless and without thought. I understand you were young, and that the woman was as much to blame as you. Especially since, being almost twenty years older, she should have had better control of her...passions."

Turning to Grant, his father scanned over him with serious eyes. "I was able to rescue my professional reputation by explaining that you were young and impulsive. However, my friendship with Dupree was ruined. We have never gotten past it."

"I am so very sorry," Grant said, meaning it. "I can speak to him if you wish."

"Too many years have passed. There is naught to be done at this point." His father shrugged. "He, too, has gone to live at the country estate. I hear he is quite unwell."

Hopefully, it meant the couple had reconciled now that they

lived together again. Grant wasn't sure what could be done if they had not. "What else can I do?" he asked, hoping his father would come up with a list. Whatever was needed, he was determined to make things better. If he was to settle down, the most important thing was to have a good relationship, once again, with his father.

"Show me that you mean what you say. I want to be proud of you, Grant. My wish is to have a son that I can boast about."

"I will do whatever it takes to make it so," Grant stated. "Whatever it takes."

His father drank deeply from the teacup and met his gaze over the rim before lowering it. "I hope so."

"Will you maintain my accounts once the ship returns?" Grant asked in a teasing tone, although he did wish his father's attention to his accounts.

"Of course." His father's response formed a lump in his throat, and he had to swallow past it.

"I do love you, Father."

"I have never doubted that, son."

The two men finished their tea and sat in comfortable silence for a bit, both enjoying their newly made peace and the time it granted them. Enjoying the familiar warmth of the study and the memories it gave him, Grant decided to avoid speaking to Wren for the moment. He needed time to consider how to explain to her about Lucinda.

He stood to leave. Grant hesitated, unsure how to part ways with his father. Thankfully the senior man stood as well. He rounded the desk and placed a hand on Grant's shoulder. "I am glad you came today."

Grant could only nod, unable to trust the ability to speak at the moment. When he walked out of the house, it was as if a boulder had been lifted from his back.

THAT EVENING OVER dinner, Evan informed Grant that Miles had stopped by. Obviously, the man was on the brink of getting almost double the amount needed from a woman who was practically buying his affection for her daughter.

"It would be wrong of him to take the money if he doesn't plan to marry her," Grant said, the situation rolling about in his mind. "What does he plan to do?"

Evan laughed. "It seems he finds it comical that he attempted to seduce the woman, and that when he mentioned the sponsorship, the woman offered double the amount and told him that the only repayment she desired was that he court her daughter."

Miles had never expressed any interest in courtship. If anything, he avoided any kind of social entanglement. Whatever rumors swirled about him were machinations of gossips' imaginations, as other than his mother or sister, he'd never escorted anyone to functions and was very rarely seen in the company of a woman to whom he was unrelated.

"I cannot imagine he would say 'yes' to such an offer," Grant said, lifting a piece of meat to his mouth.

Felicity, Grant's sister, rolled her eyes. "He may do it. The lot of you are of little honor. Once she gives him the money, he will ensure the lass is the one who wishes not to continue with any kind of entanglement with him. Poor girl."

"Did you just include me as having little honor?" Evan, her husband, pretended to be deeply insulted.

His sister didn't attempt to soothe Evan's feelings. "If not for being married to me, I shudder to think to what lengths you would go to so you could get the funding for your portion of the endeavor."

"If you remember correctly, my father paid me back earnings. I would not have had to sink too low." Evan laughed and Grant joined in, chuckling, as Felicity narrowed her eyes at Evan.

"All I am stating is that Miles Johnstone will not hesitate to take the money. He wishes to win the wager, in the smallest amount of time." Felicity turned to her husband. "What does the winner get, by the way?"

"Five percent of all our profits," Grant replied ruefully.

Evan coughed, his eyes wide. "I do not believe to have been present for that part of the discussion."

"You were actually the one who came up with it after an inordinate amount of whiskey," Grant informed him. "I am not sure anyone remembers but me."

"If it is about money and a wager, every single one of you remembers," Felicity said in a light tone. "I have a feeling, however, that not one of you will win this wager."

Grant held up a hand. "I have already won. The money I have is from one of my… er…*benefactresses*."

"You should give it back," Felicity chastised. "Honestly, Grant. I will give you the money. Evan has not touched my dowry; I have most of it. It should be almost enough. I am sure the others can come up with the rest."

He leaned forward. "You've had this money all this time and not touched it? You surprise me, sister. I would have expected you to sponsor two orphanages and purchase a building for the poor. Become the champion of hovels for orphans and the mentally insane, perhaps."

Felicity bit off the tip of a carrot, her gaze on him. "I have done some things to help others, which is why a portion of my dowry has been spent. Not that I have to give you an account. But—" she continued—"My orphanage or home for the under-privileged would be pristine, not a hovel."

"I spoke to Father today," Grant blurted, not quite sure why he decided this was a good time to bring it up, but he had to admit to being excited at the prospect of normalcy returning to their relationship. "He agreed to oversee my accounts once the ship returns."

"What?" At this, Felicity leaned forward, her inquisitive gaze taking him in. "Have you truly spoken with him? Are things settled between you two?"

"It will take time. However, I do feel as if we made progress today." Grant's chest felt lighter as he cut into the meat on his plate and popped another piece into his mouth.

"What did you say? What did he say? How did this come about?" Felicity waved her hand in his face as if he could not hear her. "Tell me everything."

Evan placed a hand on Felicity's lower arm. "Let the man eat, Love."

"He can eat later," his sister said, pushing Evan's hand away. "Speak, brother."

As the conversation with their father had not been long, repeating it to Felicity only took a moment. "Is that all?" Felicity asked, seeming disappointed. "Will we be going to our parents' for dinner soon then?"

"I am sure once Mother hears about it, she will plan something."

"I will go there first thing in the morning." It was evident his sister would insist on a family gathering. Her concentration turned to her plate, which she looked at but obviously didn't see. He was sure that instead, she was planning the menu of the meal they'd share as a family once again.

"There is something else I must inform you of," Grant said. "I have a friend. Mother has taken her on to work there at the house."

Upon his statement, both Felicity and Evan looked at him with identical frowns on their faces while they waited for him to expound. "A friend?" Felicity asked, still frowning.

"A friend?" Evan cocked an eyebrow, a smile playing at the corners of his lips. "A woman? Your friend?"

"Yes, she is a friend. She worked for Lucinda. I met her when she was sent with a missive. She is very sensible. Quite bonnie and amusing."

"You, Grant Murray, are interested in a woman who is sensible and *amusing*?" Felicity gaped at him. "Who are you?"

"I take it this woman is a maid?" Evan, who like him was raised in a wealthy household, was immediately drawn to point out the difference in stations between himself and Wren. "What can you possibly have in common? And this lass, she is aware of the nature of your relationship with Lucinda?"

At the mention of Lucinda's name, Felicity made a face akin to someone who smells a rotten fish. "I prefer not to think about *that*." She folded her hands, fingers intertwined. "Grant, you must leave the lass be. Do not take advantage of your station to play with her. Nothing good can come of it."

"I do not plan to toy with her. Instead, I am discerning how I truly feel about her, and if it is a passing fancy, I will not pursue her further."

"Ha!" Felicity's exclamation was sharp. "Men are such cretins. Exactly how do you plan to 'ascertain' how you feel? By spending time with her, giving her hope, and then—if you decide you're not as interested as you thought—walking *away*? If you wish to court her, where would you take her so that she will not feel out of place?"

"I do not have to explain things to you. I am sure we can spend time together without it being a spectacle for any of our…er…people."

"*Your* people?" Evan shook his head. "I need brandy. I do not think any of us are eating any longer. Why don't we move to the drawing room?"

"Go ahead," Felicity said. "I am going to see about our babe. I wish to play with him before he goes to sleep." As she swept past, she stopped to smile gently at Grant. "I do not mean to sound harsh, but the fact the lass is our mother's servant makes it a very delicate situation. It's an impossible one. If you want my advice, you simply must leave her be and fix your attention on someone more suitable."

BY THE TIME he went to bed, Grant was utterly perplexed. His sister and Evan were right. Where could he take Wren? If they went on an open carriage ride, she would look like a maid accompanying a gentleman for an errand. If they went to the market, or on a walk near where she lived, harmful rumors would abound. And all situations would paint her in a bad light. People would assume she'd been compromised. She'd lose her position, her livelihood.

What would the cost be for him? *Nothing.* Unable to sleep, he went to the window and peered out into the night. How exactly was he to do this? He'd definitely not thought it through.

Despite the warnings, which came as no surprise, he knew there had to be a way. Henry had married below his station, yet his marriage with Hannah was thriving. Still, Hannah's family were not from the servant class and Hannah and her parents had been friends with Grant and Felicity's family for years. Suddenly, an idea struck. His lips curved and he inhaled the night air.

There *was* a way, and he would see to it immediately.

CHAPTER FIFTEEN

T HE GLOOMY WEATHER outside matched Wren's spirits that Saturday. She'd woken to find her monthly courses had begun, bringing with them the usual aches and stiffness. She trudged to the kitchen first thing and was able—thanks to Mae's patient instructions as Wren had assisted her in the kitchen—to boil water for herbal tea that would hopefully help.

Mae found her hunched over the cup of tea, dressed for the day with a shawl over her shoulders. The older woman gave her an understanding look. "Is it this bad every month?

"Yes. It will pass in a few hours. The aches rarely last longer than the first day."

"You're in luck. There are hardly any duties to be done today. We washed the linens yesterday, and the beds have been refreshed. The sweeping and mopping have been completed." Mae added wood to the stove and stoked the fire. Then she placed a cast iron pan on the top and began cutting thick slices of bacon that she placed in the heated pan. It sizzled, and soon its delicious aroma filled the air.

"I will make the dough for biscuits. You can fry eggs in the fat once the bacon is done. I can take care of clearing and clean up. Go get some rest once the food is cooked."

She'd planned to leave early the next morning before Grant arrived and leave a simple note with the butler for him, saying that she'd gone ahead with a friend. It would suffice. For a moment, she thought about sending a message to him that day, but even though she didn't know him very well, she knew enough of him to realize he was determined and impulsive and would make sure to arrive early enough to fetch her if she gave him notice of her intentions.

Later in the day, after a short rest, she felt better and went about her assigned duties to ensure nothing would be amiss on the following day when she'd be home. Grant's mother walked in while Wren was dusting in the parlor.

"Good morning, ma'am," Wren greeted.

With a book in hand, the elegant woman went to the doorway to peer at the garden and then she turned to study Wren. "Mae informed me you were a bit under the weather this morning. How are you feeling?"

"Much better, thank you." Wren lifted a vase and moved it then began polishing the table, fully aware the woman continued to study her.

"Wren, there is something I must speak to you about."

Her stomach sank. It wasn't unexpected that along with everyone else, Grant's mother would ask that she put him off.

"Of course." Wren turned to the woman, hands clenched in front of her stomach. Her aches were back.

Mrs. Murray walked to the settee but didn't sit. Instead, she placed the book down on the side table before meeting Wren's gaze. "My son Grant has always gone out of his way to act... how should I say it? Against the norms of society."

"I understand." Wren nodded. "Whatever I can do to put him off, I will. I do not wish to cause any problems."

When the woman pressed her lips together, Wren wondered if perhaps she'd said something wrong. Mrs. Murray continued, "It is just that your actions may not be enough. I know my son. He is stubborn and if he's decided on a course of action, he is not easily dissuaded. I am sorry, Wren, but you cannot continue to work here."

Wren reached out to press a hand on the tabletop as her legs threatened to give out. "I see." She did, but it didn't make this dismissal any easier.

"It is not your fault that Grant has decided to pursue you. But because you work here, well...it brings opportunities for him to seek you out."

Wren stood unable to move, or even look at Mrs. Murray. And she couldn't prevent the string of tears that slid down her cheeks, past her chin, and dripped invisibly to the floor. "Yes, ma'am. I will pack my things and go."

The woman moved closer. "I am sorry. You are a sweet girl. Mae has a letter of recommendation, and your pay."

Just as Wren turned away, the woman touched her arm. "Wren, how do you feel about my son?"

Was it important to be honest? Her thoughts were a jumbled mess at the moment; it was impossible to give the woman a clear answer. But she tried to answer as best she could. "Your son is a wonderful, caring man who reserves judgement and seems to see all people, of every class, as equals. He is a very kind person."

Grant's mother nodded. "Yes, he is." Her eyes bored into Wren's. It was as if there was something else she wanted to say, but in the end she refrained. "You may go."

Wren raced to her small bedroom and began packing, tears flowing unabated down her face. Several times she stopped to mop them up and blow her nose. Not only had she lost her employment again and was forced to begin anew, but this time it was different. This was a wonderful place to be employed. She felt at home and enjoyed her work and the family she worked for, and the other servants. Her chest ached and she sat on the bed and covered her face with both hands. If only Grant had not declared any intentions in front of his mother.

"Oh lass." Mae appeared in the doorway and as she saw her crying, moved across the room to hug her. "I am so very sorry. You did nothing wrong."

Wren wiped at her face with the heels of her hands. "He has caused me to be let go from my positions, twice. I do not know what to think about it, except does he not realize how difficult he is making things for me? Nothing can be between us. We are much too different. Why does he not understand it?"

"The heart does not see differences," Mae replied sadly, rubbing Wren's back. "You have only been here a short time, and yet, I will miss you."

It was because it hurt so much to leave, Wren wanted to make a fast break. She didn't wait for the next day; by late afternoon, she'd hired a hackney and arrived home even before her aunt. After placing her bag of personal items on the bed, she began sorting it. Some had to be washed, other items hung or put away. It was best to keep busy and not think.

Moments later there was a knock at the front door. Wren's heart threatened to beat out of her chest. If it was Grant, it was best not to open the door.

"Delivery!" A masculine voice called out. "Delivery!"

Whoever it was did not sound familiar, so she hurried to the entrance. Perhaps her aunt expected something to be delivered. By the time she opened the door, the horse pulled wagon was already gone. A package wrapped in thick parchment had been left leaning on the wall next to the entryway.

Interesting that her aunt would purchase something that would be delivered and not only that, that it would be so elegantly wrapped with ribbons and a twig of rosemary. She picked up the box and carried it to the table. A note fluttered to the floor, landing next to her heel.

Her name was clearly written on it, and Wren immediately knew who'd sent whatever it was. The note was short:

Dearest Wren,

For Sunday afternoon.

Thinking of you,
Grant

Although she was fully aware that whatever Grant had sent her was going to be returned, Wren couldn't help but untie the ribbons and open the box. Inside, delicate tissue paper had been wrapped around several items. A pair of buttery pale blue slippers, silky stockings, and a chemise so delicate, it slid through her fingers. There was also a pair of lacey gloves that had been embroidered with tiny yellow rosettes. Under it all was the most exquisite creation she'd ever seen, a creamy, yellow-colored gown of silk with a modest square neckline. The folds of the skirt cascaded to the floor soundlessly. Without frills or ruffles, it was made to show off the wearer's attributes.

Wren slid her hand down the front of the gown and pictured what she would look like dressed in the clothes Grant had sent. No one would question them being together if she wore this, albeit it would be noticeable if she didn't have a chaperone. But it didn't matter; it wasn't to be, with or without a chaperone. With jerky movements she folded the gown and carefully replaced it, along with everything else, in the box. After one final look, she covered it all in the tissue, and rewrapped the box.

Another knock to the door made her jump.

"Delivery!"

"What now?" Wren moved to open the door where she found that the delivery man had returned. He held up a second, much smaller parcel. "I forgot to bring this, Miss."

"Wait," Wren exclaimed before he could turn away. "Please, take everything back. The person who sent these is mistaken."

"Are the items not for you?" The man looked confused. "I went to the Murrays' residence, and from there I was told to bring them here. Are you Wren?" He shifted nervously. "I am to report back to him. The gentleman was adamant that I deliver these, Miss."

It was a moment before she could reply because her anger had begun to rise at Grant's true intentions. "I will go with you to return them."

THE RIDE TO Grant's home seemed to take forever. With each passing moment, Wren became angrier. How dare he assume that he could buy her with gifts! After causing her to lose her employment—twice!—did he think she would be receptive to getting elaborate items she could never wear?

To top it off, he was Lady Robert's lover. He had no true feelings for her.

His house came into view, the sprawling estate surrounded by a perfectly tended drive lined with trees that would soon bloom. As intimidating as it was to approach such a place, Wren was too furious to feel more than a seething heat in her stomach. With the packages clutched to her chest, it was a bit tricky to climb down from the carriage, but she managed it. "Come on," she told the driver then she marched up to the door and knocked.

Clearing his throat, the driver hovered over her shoulder. "Miss, are you sure this is a good idea?"

"Be quiet," Wren snapped as the door opened. The butler she recognized from when she'd come before motioned for her to enter, again without questioning her reason for being there. It was odd, as it was obvious she was not the kind of person who visited such a place. At least, she thought, she didn't think she was, though it occurred to her that Grant might have any manner—and age!—of women visiting him.

The thought made her even angrier.

"I assume you are here to see Mr. Murray," the butler said, motioning to the sitting room.

"I am." Wren didn't move from the doorway. She was certainly not going to sit on the fancy furniture.

Just then a woman appeared at the top of the stairs with a babe on her hip. Dressed in a lovely, pale tan gown, she lifted her skirts with one hand and expertly descended the stairs. Her lips curved into a smile as she neared.

"Is there something amiss?" She looked at Wren and then the packages she held.

Her expression must have been such that the woman assumed she was upset. Wren let out a breath. "I came to return some things to Mr. Murray. I will not be long."

"I see." The woman's eyes sparkled with mirth. "I assume you are Wren."

That the woman knew her name made Wren's stomach pitch. What had Grant said about her?

"Yes, ma'am. I am." Wren managed to speak past the sudden dryness in her throat.

"Please come and sit." The woman took her arm and guided her to the sitting room. "I am Felicity, Grant's sister."

The resemblance became obvious to Wren, then. They did look a lot alike, except that Felicity's features were much softer.

"It is nice to make your acquaintance," Wren said, unsure of whether or not to curtsy. In the end, she did not.

"Sit, he is probably ensuring he's perfectly coifed before descending." Felicity shook her head. "My brother, ever the dandy."

Wren lowered to the soft chair, feeling out of place immediately.

"What did my brother do now?" Felicity asked, her gaze moving to the packages. "Oh."

Masculine voices sounded as the driver and Grant spoke. Then the sound of the door closing was followed by Grant entering the room. He stopped and gaped at seeing her, his gaze sweeping over Wren before moving to his sister. "Felicity, this is Wren Owen."

Felicity bounced the child on her lap, making no move to leave. "We have met."

"Will you give us a moment, please?" Grant said through tight lips.

"Please remain," Wren said. She'd taken an immediate liking to his sister and felt a sort of support with her in the room. Then she turned to Grant and lifted her chin before she spoke. She was not about to be the submissive servant girl anymore. Not now, anyway. She didn't work for his mother anymore, *or* his lover. "I do not have much to say to you." She stood and held out the parcels.

Although she'd reconsidered several times what she'd stay when standing before him, her mind was awhirl with so many emotions. The most challenging emotion was the way she felt insulted. The reminder that she had to be dressed in the clothes of a lady and essentially changed in order to be seen with him was a stark revelation that Grant understood their differences and especially recognized that she was beneath him. It was galling. She lifted her chin. "Your 'gift' is insulting. That you think to buy me with items makes it clear how low you consider me to yourself. Additionally, sir, these things do not make up for you causing me to lose employment yet again. *Twice* I have lost work because you *insist* on seeking me out."

His eyes rounded. "I did not know. I will speak to Mother."

"Bad idea," Felicity piped.

Grant slid a narrowed-eyed look at his sister, who acted as if she didn't notice his reaction to her opinion. He grimaced and looked back at Wren. "Wren, I am so very sorry. Surely, I can help you find other employment, something suitable."

Since he didn't take the parcels, Wren placed them on the chair. "I do not require any assistance. You cannot dress me in fancy clothes, and magically make me become someone of your class level. Don't you see? Just the fact you felt you had to do it makes our differences starkly apparent. I will not stand for it! Would you please just leave me be?" She moved toward the door. Tears threatened and it only served to make her angrier.

"I did not mean for it to be an insult," Grant said, moving sideways to impede her leaving and block her way. "It is a gift, nothing more. I am sincere in my intentions to court you, Wren."

"It can never be." She tried to step around him.

"Because you refuse to even allow us to try!" He blocked her way again.

Wren shook her head. "What I need is work so that my aunt and I can keep a roof over our heads and purchase food to eat. Fancy things will not provide those things or give me work." She fixed him with a glare. "If you would please move so I can leave!"

"Let her go, Grant," Felicity said.

His eyes met Wren's, imploring that she reconsider. "If there is anything I can do…"

"You have done enough," Wren said. She turned to look at Felicity one last time, and then rushed from the room.

"I like her," she heard Felicity say as she hurried out to find the driver waiting for her. Obviously Grant had paid the man to take her back. It would be the last thing he did for her. She'd not accept anything more from him.

CHAPTER SIXTEEN

"WHAT ARE YOU going to do?" Felicity asked, coming up behind Grant as the delivery wagon rambled away, Wren sitting next to the driver. She appeared so diminutive next to the burly man whom he'd asked to wait.

"I am not sure what I can do." He slid a look to his sister. "You heard her. She does not want anything to do with me."

For a moment, he thought Felicity would not reply. Of course, there was nothing to be said because Wren had made it abundantly clear there could never be anything between them.

"Is she right to think you and she can never be?" Felicity asked. "Are there obstacles that are too great to overcome?"

Why was she questioning him now? His mind was awhirl with what had just happened; a clear thought was hard to come by. In truth, what he wanted to do was throw something. "If she agreed to be with me, to allow me to court her, then no, there are no obstacles that are too great that we cannot work through. However..."

Felicity hit his arm. "However, a courtship between the two of you would be difficult," his sister stated. "What you need to do is propose marriage. It's obvious. She is madly in love with you and you with her. But the formality of a courtship will only make her uncomfortable."

"What?" He stared at his sister, waiting for her to admit what she'd just stated was in jest. "Wren is not in love with me..."

"Only love could bring such a passionate response to the gift.

Why did she not just send it back? Why come in person?" Felicity's eyes sparkled. "And you, dear brother. I have never seen you so affected by a woman. When you speak of her...and the way you devour her with your eyes. I have no doubt that you are deeply in love."

Grant raked a hand through his hair, not caring if it was messy. His sister was right, and he could no longer deny the truth of her words. He let his shoulders sag. "I don't know what to do."

"Must I do everything?" Felicity said to the babe who gurgled happily and swept an arm toward the now empty drive. "It's easy. Go after her. She is worth you having to grovel a bit, is she not?"

HIS HORSE WAS swift and soon the wagon came into view. Grant pulled back at the reins, slowing the horse to a trot when they came alongside.

First the driver and then Wren turned to look at him, both of their eyes widening at recognizing him.

"Stop the wagon," Grant called out.

"Don't listen to him," Wren ordered, once again looking forward.

The poor man was obviously torn; he slowed the wagon to a crawl but didn't stop completely. Grant let it be for a moment. "Wren, I must speak to you. I have something important to ask." He leaned toward her, on the side of his horse, to ensure she heard him.

"There is nothing you can say that will make me change my mind. You know I am right. It is best you go on with your life and pretend you never met me."

Grant had to direct the horse around a carriage coming past and then he rode back to position himself beside the wagon once more. "Listen to me. Please."

When Wren didn't reply, the driver gave Grant an apologetic

look. "Miss, you should at least listen to him. I have other deliveries and must speed up."

At that, Wren turned to him. "What do you wish to ask me?" The pain in her eyes made him want to jump from the horse and pull her into his arms. The visit to his house had broken her heart. She was sad.

And it was all his fault. "My question is this," he said and hesitated. Wren watched him, her gaze intent.

"Will you marry me?"

The words hung in the air. The driver pulled the wagon to a stop, which Wren didn't seem to notice. Grant pulled his horse to a halt, then dismounted and came to stand beside the wagon. "Wren, I am in love with you. Everything I've done is because I cannot imagine a day without seeing you. I have been wrong in my approach, I admit it. Please be my wife and put me out of my misery."

She stared at him agog, lips parting then closing, at a loss for words.

"Seems sincere to me, Miss," the driver interjected.

"What about Lucinda Roberts?" She lifted a brow.

"I will never return to her. I will inform her immediately that nothing will ever happen between us again."

"I believe him, Miss," the driver interjected.

To his surprise, Wren's lips twitched, then she pressed them together. With no warning and to his utter delight, she launched herself into his arms and buried her face into his neck as she clutched him tightly.

As he held her, Grant motioned for the driver to leave.

Several people walking by slowed and watched with interest as he lowered Wren to the ground. She'd yet to meet his gaze.

"Is that a yes?" Grant asked in a low tone. "Will you be my wife?"

"I think so," Wren whispered, nodding. She didn't look at him, but stared at his chest. "There is a matter we must speak about..."

"Wren, look at me." Grant lifted her face to his with gentle fingers. "I do love you."

Just then, the sound of an approaching carriage met his ears and Grant realized they stood in the middle of the road. He took Wren's arm, reached for his horse's reins, and guided both to the side of the roadway.

A pair of women who'd stopped to watch them pretended interest in each other and moved just a few feet away, still within listening distance.

"I love you too," Wren finally said. "However, I can't fathom marrying you. You and I…"

"There aren't any obstacles we cannot overcome if we face them together," Grant said, repeating Felicity's words. "Do you agree that there really aren't any that are too great?"

"I suppose," Wren finally admitted, her lips curving into a shy, pleased smile.

"Then is that a 'yes'?" he prompted, heart thundering in his chest. Never before had he wished for something more than to hear her say that *yes.*

Once again, she bit her bottom lip. Finally, releasing the moist morsel, she nodded. "Yes. I cannot believe I am saying it. But yes, I will marry you."

He fought the urge to pull her close as there were people about. Instead, he lifted her hand to his lips. "You make me a very happy man."

She turned to look toward the road. The delivery driver hadn't stayed to watch their interaction. "How am I going to get home now?"

"Walk with me," Grant said. "We have much to discuss." They walked for a few moments in silence, both of them thinking of what was to come. But then he realized where they were, and the solution seemed simple. "Would you like some tea?"

The tea shop had recently been gutted and redecorated. The new interior was decorated in shades of green and lavender. On each table, fresh flowers combined with the aroma of baking fruit tarts invited customers to linger.

Grant found a table near the window so they could look outside while enjoying their repast. Although there were a few curious glances, no one seemed to find their appearance interesting enough to take more note of in spite of Wren's protests about their differences. But he didn't choose to point this out to her; their differences weren't as great as their similarities. And they'd be even less once they were married.

His heart soared and he felt lighter than he had in a long time—maybe more so than ever.

Tea was brought as well as a tart for each of them. Wren's hands fidgeted with the hem of her shawl, so he poured.

"Are you nervous?" Grant asked gently.

"A bit, yes," she glanced at him. "I am not sure how to absorb that this is real. That you wish for us to marry."

"We both wish it. Not just me." Grant wanted to form the response as a question, but in the end made it a statement. "I do not want to influence you. If you do not wish it, then I must accept your decision. Although I fear you may lose a few more employments because I would pursue you endlessly."

When she giggled, his heart lightened. Her eyes were playful when meeting his. "I do wish to marry you more than anything I've ever wanted."

"Good." Grant waited for her to drink the tea. "When can I speak to your aunt?"

"I suppose as soon as possible. Expect many questions from her." Wren's warning was not unexpected. He would have to answer questions from his own parents as well.

"Today then." He nodded at a couple passing by their table whom he recognized. They slowed to a stop, both looking from him to Wren.

Grant stood and acknowledged them. "Anthony and Beatrice MacTavish, this is my fiancée, Wren Owen." It was the first time he'd introduced her to anyone as his fiancée or otherwise, and it felt wonderful. Until he saw the woman's expression turn to shock.

She studied Wren for a moment and then attempted but failed at a smile. "Congratulations."

Anthony, who he'd known socially, was less rigid. "You've finally been tamed. Wily fox." He shook Grant's hand and slapped him on his opposite arm.

"Nice to make your acquaintance," Wren said, her expression calm.

"Very nice to meet you," Anthony replied and then, after another slap to Grant's back continued on his way with his wife by his side.

"The news will spread like fire," Grant informed Wren. "I am afraid we must move quickly and inform my family before they hear it from someone else."

THE RECEPTION AT the Murray household was what Wren expected. The butler was formal in his greeting, his demeanor not giving away his thoughts as they walked into the house together. Once they were seated in the drawing room, the atmosphere became surreal. Wren peered through the glass in the door to the room where Grant and his mother spoke. Several times the older woman turned toward where she sat, her gaze distant as if she didn't see her there, watching them.

As much as Wren wanted to get up and run from the house, out into the street and to hide somewhere like at the shop where Laurel worked, she knew that wasn't the answer. She'd promised Grant that she would wait, that together they would face whatever came.

Her heart was torn between the love she felt for him and fear of what they'd face. A part of her wondered if she should flee and attempt to return to her simple, uncomplicated life. However, she knew that the bud of love had finally bloomed into a beautiful flower that filled her completely. She could never be happy away from Grant. A warmth spread to her that gave her courage. Just now peering through the doors to where Grant stood. Resplendent and so achingly handsome, his wide shoulders and back tapering to slender hips and powerful legs that were currently encased in boots that went over his calves.

In that moment he was facing the first of what would be many more encounters. He seemed calm, nodding as his mother no doubt listed the many reasons why they should not marry.

"Lass? What's happening?" Mae appeared with a tray. On it were a teapot, four cups and a pile of biscuits. "Why are you here?"

The woman placed the tray on a side table and moved closer, taking in the scene outside the window. "Is he speaking on your behalf so that you can work here again?"

The question made sense; the comedy of it was not lost on Wren. She wanted to laugh at the absurdity that this day had become.

"Not exactly. Grant asked me to marry him. He is informing his mother." Both she and Mae stared to where the two people had stopped talking. The matriarch straightened, as if fortifying herself, and together they turned to walk into the house.

"Oh goodness," Mae exclaimed, not making to leave. Instead, she stood next to where Wren sat as if to be there for support. That the woman remained gave Wren a sense of safety, and for it she was glad. She gave Mae a grateful look.

"Wren," Grant's mother said by way of greeting. "I hear you accepted my son's proposal of marriage." The statement was said in a tone that gave no indication of her thoughts. The woman searched her face, as if seeing her for the first time. Not that she'd been invisible to her before, but this time she was being judged on the fact that once she and Grant married, she would be part of the family.

"Mrs. Murray," Wren replied, unsure what exactly to say. The thundering of her heart and clenching of her stomach made her wonder if she'd pass out. "I love him."

For some unknown and inexplicable reason, tears pricked her eyes and Wren wiped at the corners. "I am sorry to cause you concern."

The woman lowered to sit in a chair across from her, and Grant settled next to Wren. When they sat, Mae appeared to come to life.

"I have always expected you would marry a beautiful lass," Mae murmured as she poured tea and then milk into each cup. "The best marriages are when two people truly love one another." The woman couldn't seem to stop talking. "I always told my Henry, that was why we were happy until the end."

"Thank you, Mae," Mrs. Murray finally said, bringing Mae to be silent. Mae gave Wren one last smile and left the room.

They lifted their cups and drank in silence.

"I told Mother we wish to marry as soon as possible. It will be easier for us if we marry first, and then you meet our family, our acquaintances and others."

"Easier?" Wren asked, wondering what he thought. "I think it will be the same, whether we are courting or married. Some will never accept me into their circles." She paused as the reality of this almost seemed insurmountable. She accepted it—would he? The love Wren felt for him brought a protective sense that she'd not considered. Love was unselfish, it was brave, and sacrifice was part of it. "Grant, you have to consider if that is something that will cause harm to you or your family. I would never wish to bring something that will cause harm to any of you."

"We do not have a large social presence," Grant's mother surprised her by interjecting. "Our closest friends are the Campbells. Henry married a... well, he married my daughter's best friend. The couple come from very different stations."

That her lack of social standing was to be the main obstacle made Wren sick to her stomach. "My only hesitation in this is how it will affect you," Wren said, looking to both Grant and his mother.

"Grant has made up his mind, and I assume you have as well. If you truly love my son, then you must be strong. You will be snubbed and there will be difficult moments. However, I am willing to declare that once the next item of gossip happens, the news of your marriage will pass by the wayside."

Wren studied Grant's mother trying to figure out if the woman was ready to accept their relationship. If places were traded, she would advise Grant to take time to think things through and ensure it was truly what he wanted. And, she'd tell him that she hated what he'd go through because of marrying a woman from such a low social station.

"Mrs. Murray," Wren began, "What do you think of all this? Please be honest."

The woman's smile was soft, and her gaze warmed. "I suppose I suspected how Grant felt about you before this. His admiration was evident the first time I saw him speak to you."

"What is this? What's going on?" Grant's father entered, a slight frown on his handsome face. Again, Wren's stomach tumbled with nerves.

"Grant has decided to marry," Mrs. Murray announced. "He wishes to marry Wren." She motioned to Wren. "And she's accepted."

For a long moment Grant's father took the information in. Then he stepped further into the room and stood behind his wife's chair. "I see." He scowled. "When did this come about? Were you not here when I left this morning?" he asked Wren.

Wren nodded and was about to speak, but Grant interrupted. "I just asked her this afternoon. We came immediately because some busybodies lingered as I proposed, and we wanted to be sure you learned our news from us and not from gossips."

"You must make a social appearance as soon as possible. It will cause an uproar, especially amongst certain people." Grant's mother gave him a pointed look, making Wren wonder who the "certain people" were.

"This marriage. When will it take place?" Grant's father continued to look confused. "Why was the lass working here if you were courting her? Honestly, Grant, I wonder about your ways."

Grant stood and paced. "She would not allow me to court her because of her station. I am hoping that we can marry as soon as possible. Then go forth from there."

"There is a small matter," his father stated, and a knowing look passed between the men.

Grant's mother interrupted. "The *main* matter at the moment is how we are going to deal with everything. A small ceremony at the chapel where we married would be nice. We can invite the Campbells and of course, Felicity and Evan…"

"And her family," Grant said and met her gaze with his own. His strength gave her courage. "I believe you only have your aunt and your cousin, correct?"

She nodded. "Lars, he is married and has a son."

"Both of you have small families then," his mother added. Then all three turned to a silent Wren who sat with a teacup in her hands, peering up at them.

"What do you think, Lass?" Grant's father asked.

Wren placed the cup down, picked up a napkin and dabbed it to the corners of her lips as she'd seen the older woman do. "I wish for whatever is easiest, and best, for your family, and for us."

Grant's lips curved and he looked at her as if she'd just won a major victory. "Very good."

"YOU'RE DOING *WHAT*?" Aunt Mairid showed the same lack of enthusiasm as both of Grant's parents. With a hand splayed on her chest, her rounded eyes took them in.

They were in the small kitchen where dinner preparation had been forgotten.

"Wren, are you certain? This is madness. What will you do when people snub you, and later, your bairns?"

"I will have to accept that some people will never see me as their equal. And is that so different than it's been my whole life? That's nothing different. If so, then I have lost nothing. Once we have children, then we will see."

Grant shifted in the hard chair. "I will ensure Wren is happy and always well taken care of. I assure you, she will never want for anything."

"I will be assured if you promise to keep her safe and love her always." Her aunt dabbed at her eyes with the corner of her apron and then clutched her hands on the table. "My sweet lass. I barely got to spend any time with you."

Both Wren and her aunt turned to Grant, who reached to press a hand over her aunt's. "You can be more than assured and will continue to spend time with Wren because I hope you agree to live with us."

At his words, both she and her aunt stared at him agog.

"Oh, Grant, that would be so wonderful," Wren exclaimed just as her aunt burst into happy tears.

CHAPTER SEVENTEEN

A TRIP TO the modiste was one thing Wren never thought to do, and yet here she was, accompanied by Laurel and Mae. She wore a simple gown that had been given to her by Grant's sister. Being she was a bit taller than Felicity, the hem didn't brush the top of her shoes. Despite everyone's assurances, Wren couldn't help feeling as if she played dress up in someone else's clothing. Which wasn't far from the truth.

That her fiancé's sister had to give her clothes because she didn't own anything that was anywhere nice enough to don when in Grant's company was humiliating, even now as she made her way to the modiste. It was the least expensive one she could find, since she wasn't emotionally ready to run into anyone of higher society. And she didn't want to spend too much of Grant's money. There would be announcements to come, and she would be attending social events soon enough. For now, Wren vowed to take small steps and slowly become accustomed to what was to be her new life.

They cross the cobblestone street to the side where Laurel said the modiste's shop was. There were other people walking about, mostly women carrying either baskets or bundles of whatever they'd purchased.

As they made their way beside the buildings, Wren noted the shingle hanging beside a doorway. "Belle Modiste". A carriage came to a stop on the road in front of the shop. At first Wren thought that perhaps whomever it was also planned to visit the modiste. Her blood ran cold when recognizing the emblem on the door. Lucinda Roberts' sleek carriage was the same one she'd ridden in the day she'd met Grant for the first time.

"I will speak to you!" A call came from within and then Lady Roberts peered out. The woman's steely gaze took in Wren and her companions. The footman came about and assisted the older woman from the carriage.

They flattened against the building to allow a trio of older women to pass. The women hesitated, interested in what happened. Wren mentally urged them along, but they slowed to a crawl, looking over their shoulders at what occurred.

Instead of closing the distance between where they stood and the entrance, Wren and her companions remained rooted to the spot.

The ground seemed to shrink under Wren's feet, preventing any choice of escape. Every ounce of her being screamed that she ignore the woman who stalked toward her, but Wren found it impossible.

She no longer owed the woman anything, nor was there any need to pay attention to the woman's outstretched hand, palm facing forward and calling for her to stop. However, even she understood the influence the wealthy woman had, and it was possible she could make life complicated for Grant.

"I hear things," Lucinda Roberts stated. She didn't stop in front of Wren but walked around her as if assessing her. "I have a very hard time believing what I heard."

"Lady Roberts," Wren said, bowing her head in acknowledgement. "I have no way of knowing what you heard."

The woman's upper lip twisted. "Do you not? Despite it not being announced formally, your engagement to Grant Murray is the talk of the town."

This was to be the first of many encounters Felicity—and mostly everyone they'd already told—had warned her about. Thankfully her soon to be sister-in-law hadn't just warned her, but instructed her on how to respond and what to say.

"If you wish to know if it is true, it is," Wren replied, glad her voice didn't shake. "Grant and I are to be married."

Lady Robert's gaze flickered to Wren's ringless finger, and she fought the urge to hide her hand. "I must speak to him. As a matter of fact, that is where I was heading.

"I wish you a good day then." Wren started to take a step away, but Lady Robert's hand curled around her upper arm, the grip hard, and meant to hurt her, not just stop her.

The woman leaned to speak into her ear. "There is something you should be aware of, girl. Grant is soft-hearted. In fact, he probably feels badly for you for whatever reason. Do not be fooled. A man like him can never love someone like you. We are now—and I am sure we will continue to be—lovers."

The thought was sickening, though she didn't doubt the woman's words. Wren wrenched her arm away. "We are going to be late," she said to Mae and Laurel who'd seemed as shaken as she felt. "Come, ladies."

"Ladies," Lady Roberts mocked, and chuckled without mirth. She walked back to the carriage, and moments later it lurched forward and away in the direction of Grant's house.

"Do not listen to that old cow," Mae said, bringing Wren's attention back to where they stood. "She is bitter."

Wren looked from Mae to Laurel. "I am not prepared for this." Her hand shook as she brushed it over her mouth. "I knew people would doubt us. And that—perhaps—they would find my relationship with Grant distasteful. But Lady Roberts…she *hates* me."

Laurel took her hand from her mouth and held it. "What did she say when she whispered into your ear?"

A part of it was not worth repeating until she spoke to Grant. "That he is marrying me because he felt bad and was atoning for something." Wren looked at Mae. "Could it truly be that he is going to these lengths because he caused me to be dismissed twice?"

Mae cackled. "Grant has been a confirmed bachelor most of

his adult life. If it was just that he felt bad about costing you your jobs, he would help you find another position perhaps, or try to give you money. But marriage? No, the headstrong lad marries you because he loves you. It's obvious on his face whenever he looks at you."

The words would have made her feel better if not for Lady Robert's revelation that she and Grant continued to be lovers. Was it true? She herself had witnessed his visits to her home. It had not been long since then. She remembered the other servants' whispers of shocking parties. Then, there had been the day he appeared in the room stark naked and seeking his clothing, which had been left in the most unconventional of places and not in a bedroom as they would have been for any guest. Why had she not questioned it? He'd slept there, probably with Lady Roberts.

Any sense of joy she'd had was gone thanks to the poisonous Lady Roberts. Throughout the fitting and choosing of fabrics, for the most part, she left the decisions to Mae and Laurel. The women were so engrossed in the pleasant task, they didn't seem to notice she wanted to be anywhere but there.

Wren smiled when she was expected to, and remained still, with arms out as the seamstress measured, pinned and held up samples so that the others could give the opinion on whether the colors were flattering. The only time Wren felt compelled to contradict them was when Mae held up a gaudy, floral-print fabric of huge yellow flowers. The woman laughed and admitted she was only making sure that Wren was paying attention.

In the end, six gowns were ordered, three cloaks, ten chemises, and several other items; the amount of money that would be charged to Grant's account made her head swim. They left the shop with several ready-made chemises and three dresses that would serve until her next visit.

In spite of Grant's urging, Wren refused to move into his parents' home, instead remaining with her aunt until after the wedding day. They'd not set a date for the wedding. Perhaps once that was done, she'd move into town, which would make things easier.

That day at precisely four o'clock, Grant arrived as promised to fetch her. At his request, her aunt had agreed to come along for the carriage ride.

It was a perfect day for an outing and yet, Wren could not stop thinking of what Lady Roberts had said. They climbed onto the open-air carriage and the driver encouraged the horses into a slow trot.

Within minutes, her aunt, tired from working and hurrying home, fell asleep. Wren wrapped a blanket around her. As she studied her aunt, she was glad that soon she'd no longer have to work. The older woman deserved to rest, to enjoy her later years. Except...there was Lady Roberts' confession. Grant and she were lovers.

"Has she given her notice?" Grant asked, his long-lashed gaze meeting hers. Dressed in dark brown, his perfectly tailored suit brought out his olive complexion and dark hair. He was so devastatingly handsome, she thought, she could stare at him for hours.

"I believe so, yes." Wren busied herself by looking around at the passing scenery. They were to ride in the country that day to spend time getting to know each other more. Except, what if it was false; what if he didn't love her as he'd said? What if their time apart he spent his time pleasuring and taking pleasure from another woman? If that was so, Wren didn't want to get to know him better. If at all. Not if the wretched woman's words were true, and she was horrified to find out if they were.

"Is there something wrong?" Grant reached for her hand, taking it in both of his. "You are very quiet. Did something happen at the modiste?"

"The modiste was fine. I feel strange spending so much on clothing."

"You will need it. I do not mind at all." He looked away for a moment as if in thought. "Soon I am to come into a large fortune.

It will allow me the opportunity to give you your heart's desires."

The desires of her heart weren't something that could be bought. In fact, she was struggling to keep her heart from breaking. The question she longed to ask him lingered on the tip of her tongue and she fought not to let it emerge. But, she knew, it had to be spoken. "There may not be a wedding," she finally stated.

His gaze flew to her, his eyes widening. "What?"

"Are you still Lady Roberts' lover? I cannot marry you if you continue to be with another woman." Her voice cracked on the last words and Wren pulled her hand from his. "I saw her today and she admitted it to be true."

"Ah." Grant let out a long breath, his gaze falling to his lap. "I had hoped not to have to speak of this so soon."

The carriage had to stop. Wren wanted to scream to the driver to take them back so he would stop. Most of all, she didn't want to continue on a drive, a romantic gesture, while her fiancé admitted that he had a lover, and that he did not plan to change his roguish ways. Instead, he expected her to accept it.

But she wouldn't. No matter how much she thought she loved Grant, there was no way she'd allow herself to be in a marriage where her husband was unfaithful. It was going to be hard enough with their differences in social class. But that was something she could overcome. This betrayal, however, she refused to accept or condone.

"There is time to cancel the modiste. I can find work with Lars, my aunt's son. Perhaps he can help me. We do not have to speak about this." If they did, her heart would shatter, and she would not be able to stop her tears.

Her aunt stirred as Wren's voice had risen, but she settled back with a soft snore escaping her lips.

Her aunt! Tears threatened to spill at the realization she'd have to break her wonderful aunt's heart too. She'd spoken of little else than their upcoming move and constantly wondered about the kind of house they would live in. It had been the topic she'd hoped to talk with Grant about that day.

Grant took Wren's hand and wouldn't allow her to remove it as he said, "Lucinda and I *were* lovers. I have not attended any functions or events with her since the day I walked into the sitting room, and you saw me there. I am sorry she upset you." Grant's face was hard. "She had no right."

Wren studied his face, trying to ascertain if he *did* speak the truth. "She gave me the impression your...er...assignation remains."

A muscle on Grant's jaw moved as he clenched it. "She lied. I give you my word. I cut all ties with her, and all the others, the moment I realized I only wished to be with you."

Her breath caught in her throat. What was he inferring? "O-others?"

Grant raked his hand through his hair, his gaze moving to her aunt. "Yes, others. I must tell you the truth about myself, though you may refuse to marry me after. I don't want to tell you, but I promised myself not to go into this union without being completely honest with you."

He waited for her to say something, but Wren was at a loss. Too many questions whirled in her head that it made it impossible to formulate words. He seemed to realize this and continued, "Most everyone knows what kind of man I am. It is public knowledge that I benefit from... spending time with women. Mostly wealthy older women who are widowed or lonely. I served as a companion, giving them attention they no longer could receive because their husbands are gone or because they're no longer considered desirable because of their age or...for whatever reason. I am not proud of what I've done. It caused a rift between my family and me, but, when I was asked to leave my home, I found it to be an easy way to have money and write, which is what I always wished to do. To write."

"Were these women aware of the others?" Wren wasn't sure why she asked that instead of other more pertinent questions. How could he do it? Was it something men in the upper level of society did? Surely it was frowned upon. After all, in the end, he was selling himself, was he not?

CHAPTER EIGHTEEN

T HE LOOK ON Wren's face, part shock and part disgust, was exactly why he'd dreaded having to tell her the truth about himself. He should have informed her fully before proposing. Instead, he'd allowed himself the hope of never having to reveal who he was and what he did.

It was her right to know, and yet Grant had hoped he didn't have to tell her the truth until after they were married. Yes, it would have been unfair to her, and yet he was being selfish. His fear of losing her was overwhelming. He couldn't think to withstand it.

"Yes. The women are aware I am not interested in a relationship other than what I could bring to their beds. That included Lucinda."

She tugged her hand from his grasp, and while he wanted to hang on to it, he let her go. "Understand, Wren. I never took advantage of them. And sometimes their only need was for an escort to social events."

"But you did have more intimate relationships with most of them. Did you not?"

Grant nodded. "Yes. I did. I am not proud of it. I realized a long time ago that one day I would regret my lifestyle and I feared when it would happen. But then I met you and I knew it was time to start anew. Twice recently I have had the difficult conversations I feared. With my father, and now... with you."

Wren looked away. He was certain she did not see the passing scenery, nor did she notice the warm breeze that only happened in Scotland on rare occasions. The sky was a bright blue, however, in that moment, he almost wished for a gray one with heavy, dark clouds that threatened to rain and matched his mood. And hers.

"Will you forgive me?" he finally asked. "Please do not leave me." His throat constricted. "I promise you, I have not seen any woman but you since the day when you went to work for my mother."

It seemed like forever, but finally Wren turned to him. Unshed tears filled her eyes, and she studied his face. An angry expression crossed her features. "For all your money and social standing, it seems you are of a much lower station than I am."

He was a whore. She didn't have to say it out loud for him to know what she thought.

"So, you will not marry me then?"

Wren stared straight ahead without replying.

"I will take you home," Grant said. His heart was broken and filled with disgust, but even to his own ears his voice was without emotion. "You can decide when we will make the announcement that everyone that we have decided not to marry."

Wren was quiet. She sat rigid next to him making it hard to decipher what she thought. But maybe he didn't have to—she was filled with disgust, as he would be. As anyone would be.

Upon reaching her house, the carriage came to a stop, and he climbed down to help her drowsy aunt down.

When he lowered Wren to the ground, he held her in place. "Mrs. Owen, can I speak to Wren in private for a moment?" he asked her aunt.

The woman gave him a warm smile. "Do not linger." She walked around to the side where the door was.

Wren had yet to look at him. He lifted her face with his index finger under her chin. "Promise me to think things through. I am aware that you deserve a much better man. Wren, I promise to be that man. To become a better person, to earn your trust and admiration once again. If only you will have me."

He swallowed and fought not to beg more. It would kill him if she walked away without giving him hope.

"I cannot give you a reply right now." She searched his face as if looking for the man who asked her to marry him and not finding him. "I apologize for my outburst earlier. I have no right to judge."

Grant nodded. "Can I call on you tomorrow?"

"No. I will come to you. I need time." Wren walked around him and went inside.

He stood next to the carriage debating whether or not to go to the door and explain more. Or try to explain again. Except, what could he say? That he was worthy of her. Except what she'd said had cut him to the core. It was true. He was lower in status than she when one considered that he indeed sold his body in exchange for a life of luxury.

Grant had never been proud of it, but neither had it bothered him as it did now. Of course, people in his circles suspected, but he came from a wealthy family, so it was not obvious that he had no money of his own. Then again, he had amassed a good amount of money that he'd saved, not enough for sponsorship of the ship, but enough that he could provide for Wren until the ship returned.

"Sir?" The driver peered down at him. "Permission to speak freely?"

He nodded and looked up to the older man. "Of course."

"Allow her time to consider things. If you demand to speak to her right now, she will rebuff you."

Without a word, he climbed back onto the carriage not seeing anything other than the expression on Wren's face when he'd disclosed the sins of his past. For the first time in his life, Grant wished that he could turn time backward, change so many things.

However, if not for being Lucinda's lover, he would have never met Wren.

Once arriving home, he stormed past the foyer and into the

sitting room where he poured a generous portion of whiskey into a crystal glass. The fiery liquid trailed down his throat and into his stomach and he closed his eyes.

"For a man who's recently engaged, you do not look very happy." Evan's deep voice brought him out of his revelry. "Has something happened?"

He met his brother-in-law's gaze. "Lucinda confronted Wren. Told her we were lovers, among other things."

"That could not have gone over well," Evan said. He sat in a chair holding a book, a glass of whiskey at his elbow, atop a small table. Distraught, Grant hadn't noticed him when he first entered the room.

"No," Grant admitted. "It did not. I am not sure she will marry me."

He lowered to a chair and stretched out his legs. "I do not blame her."

"You love her." Evan's statement hung in the air.

"Of course I do. With all my heart." Grant took another drink. "What good will it do me?"

Evan shrugged. "It will give you the courage to fight for her. To show her that you are indeed a changed man who will be faithful."

"How the hell will I prove that?" Grant snapped. "I have no idea what she is thinking right now. No—I do. She is thinking I am no better than a whore."

Evan put his book aside and looked at him for a long moment. "I am sorry this happened."

To top off the already dreadful evening, Grant blinked away tears of frustration. "Thank you."

"Tomorrow you will feel better and have a clear head," Evan said, looking pointedly at the glass in Grant's hand. "If need be, recruit Felicity to help. I am sure she will have good ideas."

As he climbed the stairs, leaving the half-empty glass behind, Grant considered how his sister could help. Perhaps he'd also get Henry's wife, Hannah, to help as well. Surely Wren would understand that like both Henry and Evan, he too could change from a rogue to a devoted husband.

Because he'd promised Wren he wouldn't call on her, Grant waited an excruciating two days to finally contact Wren. He sent a note via the coachman asking her to meet him and was overjoyed—or as overjoyed as he could be when she replied affirming that they could meet. He hoped it would be so that he could marry his beloved, and not lose her because of his own lack of foresight.

CHAPTER NINETEEN

FOR TWO NIGHTS, Wren had barely slept, vacillating between feeling horrible for what she'd said to Grant and angry that she'd fallen in love with a man like him who slept with women in exchange for money, clothes, finery. How could she ever get past the pictures in her mind of him with not just Lucinda Roberts but with so many other faceless women? If they married, she would encounter the women who'd slept with her husband. It was even possible she would speak to them without knowing they'd been his lovers before she claimed him as her own.

They would have known him intimately. Just thinking about it brought angry tears. No, not just angry, but a mixture of so many other things. Outrage, hurt, jealousy, as well as a deep resentment that no one had informed her about.

"You remain cross with me?" her aunt asked when Wren walked into the kitchen.

Wren stopped, not expecting her to be home. "I did not expect you'd be home today."

"Well, I am," her aunt said, standing. "I couldn't very well leave you alone in this state."

"You knew he was Lucinda Roberts's lover and never told me." Wren couldn't help the sharpness in her tone. "Why?"

Her aunt looked at her, taking her in. "You are a pure girl. I suspect never kissed before Grant." She waited until Wren nodded. "The world is filled with so many things that you are not aware of, lass. Grant Murray, like his friends, is a rogue. The thing is that high society plays by a different set of rules. If I am to be honest, they live a life that is much less inhibited than ours."

"Do you not find it shocking?"

"Of course I do." Her Aunt Mairid motioned to a chair and Wren sat. She continued explaining, "I know that Grant visited on occasion, mostly during Lady Roberts' gatherings. We all suspected that all manner of activity took place. It was odd, especially because most of the servants were sent away during her parties. Only a few remained and they were sworn to secrecy. Which in itself made people question what occurred—what was so bad that secrets needed to be kept?"

"That is why he was naked that day." Wren covered her face. "How could I be so stupid?"

Her aunt made a sympathetic sound. "You should give Grant a chance. He has promised to be only yours."

"What of all the others, Aunt? Do I ignore that he's been intimate with women in exchange for—"

Her aunt interrupted. "Yes. You ignore it. Men are held to different standards than women. Especially in the higher levels of society."

"How is that fair?" Wren asked in a raised voice.

Her aunt shook her head. "It is not. However, men have fewer risks than women. They do not have to worry about the possibility of pregnancy. It is much more dangerous for women to be less inhibited. A child could come from it. Disgrace comes from that, and a loss of self-respect resulting in being ashamed."

"Ashamed?" Wren asked, truly intrigued. "Why should a woman be ashamed for what men are prideful about?"

Her aunt let out a breath. "We should not be, dear lass. However, women are made to feel that way by the rules of this world we live in."

What her aunt said was true. Yet she was not sure how she'd feel about Grant when seeing him again. Her response as to whether she'd marry him or not would come from how she felt. The answer would only come to her upon seeing him.

In the note he'd sent, Grant had assured her there would be others there and that whoever would be present would represent his family.

"Aunt Mairid, will you come with me today?" Wren asked. "I would like you to come."

Her aunt smiled. "Of course, I will. But I want you to know that I think you should not marry him unless you are absolutely certain. No matter what, we will be fine."

It was left unsaid that her aunt had already given notice that she'd leave her position at Lady Roberts'. Seeming to read her mind, her aunt added, "Do not worry. Lars has been after me to quit for months. He will ensure we have a roof over our heads and food on the table."

Well, that was one thing she no longer had to worry about. No matter what, her aunt would be fine, and better, she wouldn't have to work anymore. "Very well. I will do my best to maintain an open mind and hear what Grant has to say. I love him dearly, but I am not sure I can move forward."

Her aunt squeezed her hand. "Follow your heart, dearest."

GRANT SENT HIS carriage to fetch her, and upon arriving at the estate where he lived with his sister and her husband, Wren was sure her heart was beating so hard it was audible. It took a few breaths before she could alight. Waiting for her to help her down was Grant.

The sun on his brown hair showed off the lighter highlights that she'd not noticed before. The already fast beating of her heart seemed to skip several at his hand taking hers. The entire time, he looked into her eyes as if trying to find the answer to what would happen from that day forward.

Wren wondered if he saw uncertainty because up to that point, she'd yet to make up her mind about anything. She'd be hard-pressed to give more than *yes* or *no* answers to any question.

"You are beautiful today," he said as he took in her pale blue gown, another of his sister's loans, and her hair. Although distressed, she'd taken extra time with her coif and fixed it in the simple swept-up style that she'd seen other women wear.

As always, when she looked at Grant and then at his huge home, she expected to feel out of place, inadequate. Strangely, she did not. Instead, especially after her aunt's revelations, she felt more than adequate to be there. Not that she held herself in higher regard than the people inside, but that she now knew they were not better than she was.

"Shall we?" Grant said, offering his arm. "My sister is inside and insists on speaking to you before allowing us privacy to talk." He guided her up the stairs to the front door where the footman had already escorted her aunt.

It was sweet the way her aunt's eyes sparked with curiosity at seeing the inside of such a grand home. It was smaller than Lady Roberts', however, it was more elegant.

Once inside, they stepped into the marble-floored foyer where her aunt took a moment to admire the sweeping staircases, one to each side of the corridor between them, the polished floors gleaming.

"They await in the sitting room," Grant said, leading them there.

Wren was surprised to see not only Grant's sister, and her husband, but three other people there who she didn't recognize.

Felicity stood and held her hands out in greeting. When Wren grasped her hands, she pulled her forward into the room. "I wish to introduce you to our little group."

First, she motioned to her husband. "This is my husband, Evan McLeod." The attractive tall man bowed in acknowledgement. Felicity continued, motioning to a couple consisting of a beautiful brunette and a light-haired man, with plush lips, heavily lashed eyes, and eyebrows that seemed to be painted by an artist. He had to be the most beautiful person she'd ever seen. "I present

Henry and Hannah Campbell. Henry is a lifelong friend of Grant and Evan."

A dark-toned man sat leisurely in a chair, his long legs stretched out in front of him. He was elegant and seemed the most reserved of the group. He studied her with half-closed eyes, seeming to not find any fault by the arching of one brow, as if in approval. When Felicity came to him, he stood. Felicity introduced him by saying, "This handsome creature is Lord Miles Johnstone. Also, a lifelong friend of my husband and brother."

His Lordship's movements were graceful as he took Wren's right hand and brought it up to his lips. The light kiss felt intimate, especially when his chocolate brown eyes lifted to hers. "I am very pleased to meet you." His voice was silky like velvet and Wren considered that no woman could possibly be immune to it. A moment later, however, he was once again in the same chair with the distracted expression of someone who preferred to be anywhere but there.

"Please sit," Felicity said after Grant introduced her flushed aunt to the group. He led Wren to a settee and then stood behind her, while Felicity showed her aunt to a chair.

There was a beat of silence before Felicity, obviously the group's spokesperson, said anything. She started by smiling at Wren. "Hannah and I wished to speak to you. I asked the men to join us just for a moment so that you can know who Grant's closest friends are."

Henry met her gaze. "He is a reformed scoundrel, I assure you. My friend is loyal and steadfast."

Behind her, Grant groaned. "This is not an inquest. No need to say all that." When she turned to look up at him, his cheeks were pink.

"I second what Henry said," Lord Johnstone said, standing again. "However, I expect—as his friends—we would say something like that. Therefore, I will allow the ladies to reassure you."

Evan motioned to the men, and they filed out, Grant last after giving her shoulder a light pat.

"Goodness. They seem to take the air out of the room," Hannah spoke for the first time, fanning herself. She looked to Wren and then away, obviously a shy person by the way she seemed to regret her outburst.

"I agree," Wren said, and the woman smiled brightly.

A maid walked in with a tray of small goblets of amber liquid. They each took one, her aunt eyeing hers with suspicion. "Now, let us have some honeyed mead. My mother purchased some and sent it over. I suppose she expected we'd need it after I told her about you and Grant," Felicity explained.

They drank it slowly, and Wren had to admit the sweet liquid did relax her. Or perhaps it was that Grant had left the room, and she could breathe easier.

"How are you feeling?" Hannah asked. "I hope you do not feel ambushed. That was not our intention."

Wren placed her empty goblet on the tray the maid had left on a center table. "I understand why you all came. You care for Grant and wish for him to be happy, but in all honesty, I am not sure how I feel."

"We *do* want Grant to be happy," Felicity affirmed. "We wish to speak on Grant's behalf before you decide whether to marry him or not. Not to make excuses for him because no justification can be made for his actions in the recent past. But to talk to you about the man he is now, and we expect to be in the future."

Her aunt sighed, holding up the empty goblet. "Is there more?"

Hannah giggled. "I will have another with you." She lifted the glass decanter from the tray and refilled their glasses. Both Felicity and Wren declined another serving.

It was best to speak frankly, so Wren let out a breath. "I worry that I will not be able to get past the thought of him with other women. The fact that they will be about and part of social events and that they will know who I am, but I will not be aware of who they are."

Felicity nodded with understanding. "The both of us can relate. We both married rogues with a rather checkered past. Being that I've known Evan, Henry, and Miles for so long, I've seen them all with different women. I am sure there are women with whom Evan has had interludes that I am not aware of, and I choose not to give them importance or allow them to interfere in our marriage by thinking about them."

The words made sense, but Wren wasn't sure to be strong enough.

"When I fell in love with Henry," Hannah began, "One of the things I had to know was if he was going to change and become a good husband. I needed to trust that he would, and so far, he has."

Felicity nodded. "They are worthy men, with noble hearts. Unfortunately, they have lived the carefree bachelor's life that men often do. My parents and I have been praying that Grant finally settles down and we despaired of it ever happening."

The pretty woman leaned forward and met Wren's gaze. "Believe me when I tell you that my brother has never been in love before, and since meeting you, the change in him has been drastic. He truly loves you and will do anything for you— including walking away if you cannot get past this."

Unexpectedly, tears trickled down her cheeks and Wren wiped them away. The way the people in the house had converged to do this for Grant was wonderful. They cared for him dearly and would be there to support him if she decided against the marriage.

"Lass." This time, her aunt spoke. "Do you love him?"

Wren nodded. "I do."

"Enough to fight for him?" her aunt asked.

She hesitated. Was she strong enough? In the last months, she'd left the home she'd known forever and had found herself in situations unlike anything she'd ever known. Through it, she'd known it was what one did to survive. This was no different. She needed to be strong and to fight her way through it. "I will speak with him," Wren said, standing. "Do you know where he is?"

Felicity stood and nodded. "Come." She walked with her to the arched doorway of the parlor. "In the garden."

As she walked toward the same doorway she'd been outside of the day she'd met him, she noted that the furnishings were sparse on that side of the house. Only an occasional table, or a pair of chairs flanking a sideboard with a mirror over it. There were a pair of portraits on the opposite wall, people she assumed were Evan's ancestors.

The garden doors came into view, sun streaming into the house. Grant was not in view, so she went to them, opened the doors, and walked outside.

He stood looking out to the back of the house, his hand resting atop the waist-high brick wall. Fully dressed in his morning suit, he looked every bit a gentleman.

"Grant," Wren said, watching as he turned, his gaze flying to her. With purposeful strides, he was immediately at her side. "I was beginning to wonder if you'd gone." He took her hand and led her to the table where they'd shared a meal.

She felt so very different now. "Please sit."

"I do not wish to sit. I've been sitting too long."

It was hard to read his expression. He was wearing a mask of composure she was sure he'd donned so as not to allow her to know what he thought. It was hard to look at him, so she looked away, at the flowers she always enjoyed. Butterflies floated from one bloom to the next, and she followed their progress for just a moment.

Finally, Wren looked up at him. "The other night when you told me about your past, why did you tell me about the others? You could have just admitted about Lucinda Roberts and left it at that."

His Adam's apple bobbed. "Whether one or more women, they are a part of my life. If you are to marry me, I wish for you to know everything."

It was hard to think past the fact that she wanted Grant to

hold her, to feel his strong body against hers. But that wouldn't solve this challenge they faced forever, it would only bring her peace for a short while. Once she stepped out of his arms, the problem would still exist.

"Even until arriving, I had not made up my mind yet."

His calm façade fell, replaced with an expression of dread and sorrow. He nodded. "Of course. I realize it is not easy."

A heaviness settled across her shoulders, and she fought to push it away. Wren opened her mouth, unsure of what she'd tell him. Then, looking into his gaze, she knew. "Grant, I will marry you."

She waited for a moment of panic or denial, or a feeling that she'd made the wrong decision, but there was none. Instead, it felt right. She felt right.

At first, he stared at her as if not understanding what she'd said. Then he let out an audible breath and swept her into his arms. "Oh, thank God." With her head on his chest, the thundering of his heart echoed in her ear and immediately she felt as if a heavy sodden cloak was removed from her and replaced with lightness.

"Thank you." He whispered. "I love you."

Wren looked up at him. "Kiss me. Assure me with a kiss that everything will be well."

His mouth covered hers, and he kissed her like never before. This was not a kiss of passion, but one of claim. He was claiming her as his, and as his tongue parted her lips, she gladly allowed it, enjoying the intrusion and reveling in the strength of his embrace.

"Wren," his deep voice pulsed through her when he spoke against her ear, the breathless word saying so much more than an entire declaration of love. The huskiness was followed with a sniff. He'd been expecting her to leave, to refuse to marry him. And he was not altogether wrong, because in her mind, she could not fathom marrying him because of his past. However, when seeing him surrounded by the people who loved and supported him and then seeing the sadness he tried bravely to hide, she could not walk away.

"I love you," Wren said, sliding a hand up and down his back. "I cannot live without you."

He cupped her face with both hands. "I cannot fathom my life without seeing you every single day. I am so very sorry…"

"No more talk of that. Let us put it all behind us and move forward."

She thought he smiled, but he kissed her then and she forgot about everything other than the taste of the man she loved and her impatience to be more intimate.

"Can we marry immediately?" she asked.

"Is tomorrow soon enough?" Grant asked between kisses.

CHAPTER TWENTY

THREE DAYS LATER, they were married in the flower garden at Evan and Felicity's house, surrounded by the same people who'd been in the sitting room as well as Grant's parents. Lars and his wife Bettina were also there, as were her Aunt Mairid, and her friends Martha and Laurel, who kept staring at Miles Johnstone and blushing furiously.

With an empire waist, long sleeves, and a square neckline, her wedding dress was simple and elegant. Wren wore a pearl necklace and matching earrings, gifts from Grant's mother.

Although trembling, Wren managed to hold the bouquet handed to her by Felicity. "I am so very pleased for you and Grant," she said, hugging Wren. "Make each other happy."

Wren wondered if she'd faint from an inability to breathe. She took shallow breaths, but it seemed as if not enough air entered her lungs.

As she walked past the guests on Lars' arm, she looked forward. Grant stood next to the vicar. Her handsome soon-to-be husband's hair was damp, the ends curling on his collar. His gray ensemble molded to his body, showcasing his wide shoulders and powerful thighs. That he was to be hers was hard to grasp.

A jolt of panic struck, and Wren hesitated. Then their gazes met, and she found herself lost in his eyes and everyone disappeared until there was only him. Her breathing instantly calmed.

Upon coming to stand next to him, he took her hand in his and leaned to speak into her ear. "Calm down, little dove.

Remember, I love you."

Wren took a deep breath, and then she looked to the vicar.

The vicar spoke in low tones, and they repeated the vows he gave them, Grant with assuredness, while Wren's voice cracked with emotion.

When the vicar asked for rings, gold bands were produced and slipped onto each other's fingers. Wren was pleasantly surprised that hers fit perfectly. When pronounced husband and wife, Grant pulled her into his arms and kissed her soundly. She was sure her cheeks were bright red when he released her, but she didn't care. She was Grant Murray's wife.

It was the happiest moment of her life.

There was a loud sniff and Wren turned to find her aunt looking up to the sky. She followed the woman's line of sight, noting rays of sun streaming from the clouds and she felt her family's presence. They'd come to wish her well.

EVERYONE MOVED INSIDE to the dining room, which had been decorated with large vases of fresh flowers. The wedding meal was resplendent; meats, vegetables, breads, cheeses, and pies of every variety were served by the efficient staff. Wren had expected not to have an appetite, but the opposite was true. Every dish that was presented was more tempting than the last and she tasted a bit of each.

The sun had fallen by the time they'd finished the meal and toasts were made.

"It is time for you to leave the festivities," Aunt Mairid informed Wren. "Go on upstairs." Her aunt hugged her tightly. When they pulled back, tears slid down her aunt's face. "Your mother would be so very happy today."

"Good night," Lars and his wife chorused, and then they and her aunt left to travel back to town.

Across the room, Grant laughed at something someone said, then sensing her gaze, he turned and immediately walked to where she stood at the bottom of the stairs. Without a word, he lifted her into his arms and carried her up the stairs while the guests cheered and clapped below.

ONCE INSIDE A very masculine bedchamber, he lowered her to stand. Wren wasn't sure what to do. Thankfully Grant took over, first pulling her against him, his mouth covering hers with soft kisses.

"You were resplendent today, Mrs. Murray," he whispered in her ear. "I cannot wait to make you mine."

The feel of his warm lips over hers, pressing on the corners of hers, then traveling down the side of her neck, his tongue licking circles. A soft moan erupted as she clung to him.

Trailing a path to her shoulder then back up to nibble on her ear sent tendrils of desire through Wren. It was so very nice, these new sensations that stirred within her, then up and down her body.

His mouth never leaving her body, moving provocatively to her throat, Grant managed to untie the laces that held her dress in place. In a haze, she noted the dress slipping off her shoulders, past her hips, and falling to the floor. She should have been shocked, or at least worried about the gown, but all she was fully aware of was that she wanted to be taken by this man.

Finally, he stepped back. There was a curve to his lips as he slid his coat off, then his vest, and finally he unbuttoned and removed his shirt. When his hands went to the waistband of his trousers, Wren stared in astonishment. She'd seen him naked before and knew he had a beautiful body, but tonight, it was so very different, because he was her husband and now his body belonged to her. With hungry eyes, she watched closely as he bent and quickly did away with his stockings, then finally removed his trousers.

Wren swallowed, her gaze pinned to his aroused member. *That* she had definitely not seen before.

"You caused this," he said, taking himself in hand. "I am aroused at the thought of being with you."

Sleek and graceful, moving as she imagined a panther after prey moved, he closed the distance, and taking hold of the hem of her chemise, pulled it off, over her head. Grant's sharp intake of breath was followed by him sliding both hands down her sides. "You are perfection."

Wren was aware men preferred full breasts like hers, a slender waist, and soft rounded hips. Her body seemed to please Grant, and she was dizzy with happiness.

"I am yours and you are mine," he murmured as he lifted her once again, this time walking to the bed and placing her upon it.

He climbed onto the bed and lay next to her. They rolled to their sides and faced each other. Wren wondered why he didn't proceed. She wanted more kisses and caresses. The desire to be his consumed her.

"Do you know what happens in the marital bed?" he asked, his eyes boring into hers. "Between a man and a woman?"

Wren nodded slowly. "I know that we are to join. With our bodies."

"Do you understand how?" he persisted.

If the man continued to question her, she may as well go to sleep. "I imagine your member will do something."

A smile threatened at the corners of his lips. Then he pulled her closer and kissed her. His hand traveled down her body, and she shivered. "We will join. My staff..." he paused and slid his hand between her legs.

Shocked at the touch, she pushed her legs together, but then forced herself to relax.

To her amazement, Grant trailed kisses to her breast, then took one tip into his mouth and teased it with his tongue.

It was the most wonderful feeling, when he suckled at it, then moved to the other breast. On her back now, she arched into him, wanting him to continue. Awareness of where his hands were returned when he palmed her sex.

Grant took her mouth again, and at the same time, his finger slid between the folds of her sex and Wren's eyes flew open as heat pooled at her core. When he began circling the nub in the center with his finger, she grabbed his shoulders, not sure if she wanted him to continue or stop.

"Close your eyes, feel it," Grant whispered. "My staff will enter you here." One of his fingers slid into her, while the other continued to stroke her to distraction.

Like water tumbling from a waterfall, rivers of desire coursed through her to the very center, and she shuddered. Her body was aflame and floating at the same time as she cried out Grant's name.

"Oh. Oh," she repeated several times, unable to form any other words. "Whatever he'd done was magic. If only it would continue.

Grant climbed over her; so much skin against her already sensitive body made it hard to figure out what he did. Just as she was about to ask, once again he took her mouth, and all was forgotten.

The sensation of being stretched as his staff prodded against her was strange. Wren squeezed her eyes shut, unsure of what would happen. But he was relentless with his mouth, licking down the side of her neck, nipping lightly at the very sensitive base of her throat. *"Mm...mm."* She was about to float away when suddenly a piercing pain broke through everything, and she cried out.

"Shhh," Grant murmured and drove in deeper, and after a moment, it didn't hurt. The throbbing subsided almost as fast as it came, and she let out shallow breaths.

Pushing his face up, Wren met his gaze. "What happened? Will it always hurt?"

He shook his head. "No, just this once. I tore your maiden-head."

"So are we finished?" Wren asked, noting his breathing was more like pants.

"No, my beauty. We are not. Relax around me." Being that it felt as if he filled her completely, Wren wasn't sure how he expected her to relax, but she did her best.

"Kiss me," Grant instructed, and she pulled him down for a kiss. At first, the kiss was tentative, testing, but soon, it deepened, his tongue probing, his hands caressing her body.

Wren wanted to touch him too. "Can I touch you?"

His deep chuckle was nice, and he nodded. "My body is yours."

The statement sent a shiver through her; well, there was that and the fact he was moving his hips forward and backward, his staff sliding in and out of her. Wren ran her hands down his back, stopping at the swell of his bottom, unsure she dared go there. It was hard to concentrate with him moving.

Her eyelids fluttered shut without her trying to keep them open, and she sighed happily, enjoying his movements. The faster he moved, the more she wanted; it was as if he dangled a carrot just out of reach and she was determined to grab it.

"Faster, more." Wren dug her fingernails into the small of his back. "Yes."

Suddenly she crested, her entire body seeming to burst into pieces, and this time she covered her mouth with her hand as screams of ecstasy could not be stopped. Grant continued the wonderful onslaught until he, too, suddenly let out a hoarse cry and shook as he also became lost.

Slick with perspiration, breathing harshly, Grant rolled to his back, bringing her with him, and kissed her. "I love you so very much. It has never been like this."

Wren would have replied, but she clung to the passionate abyss, her body so taut she wondered if the sensations would ever stop. It was as if her body continued to climb.

Seeming to understand, Grant rolled her to her back and then he once again reached between her legs. Wren wasn't sure what he did until his finger circled the special place. She arched and curled her fingers around the blankets.

When he stroked her one more time, all her strength left, and she grabbed the bedding harder, fearing what would happen. He trailed his mouth next to her ear. The flicks of his tongue and the heat of his mouth were more than she could take, and several seconds later she crested with so much force, that stars formed behind her lids.

"Grant!"

"Can you hear me?" The urgency in Grant's voice made Wren open her eyes.

"Why do you ask?" she murmured, blinking up at him as he slowly came into view.

"I think you fainted." Grant kissed her lightly. "How do you feel?"

Wren inhaled deeply, lips curving. "I feel as if I will never be the same again. If I had known how wonderful marital relations were, I would have married years ago."

"It is a good thing you did not then." Grant grinned proudly. "It is only when two people feel so strongly about one another that making love becomes so much richer."

Wren touched the tip of his nose with her finger. "It will be hard each day to wait until bedtime."

At this Grant chuckled. "You may wish to wait a day before we join again. You may be a bit tender. But once your body adjusts, my love, we don't have to wait until bedtime. We can make love as often as I can make it happen." He kissed her. "I believe that will be several times a day. Or more. And there are other ways we can pleasure one another. But I'll share those with you on another day. After all, we have the rest of our lives."

Despite fighting it, the yawns won, and she admitted to herself to be tired from the long day.

"In the morning, we have much to discuss."

Grant nodded. "Until then, rest, my love." He brought her closer, his arms possessive around her. Within minutes, her new handsome husband was fast asleep.

But sleep didn't come easily for Wren. She was in a strange room and in bed with a very naked, handsome man. How could she keep from touching him? Tentatively, she ran her hand over his chest, enjoying the feel of taut skin over the hard planes. Letting out a long sigh, she snuggled closer, wondering what exactly the other ways of intimacy entailed.

CHAPTER TWENTY-ONE

WREN WOKE TO find Grant dressing; he stood in front of a full-length mirror, his eyes moving to meet hers in the glass.

"Good morning," he turned and came to the bed, and placed a lingering kiss on her lips.

"I overslept," Wren said, sitting up and pushing disheveled hair away from her face. "Goodness, I normally braid my hair before sleeping."

He picked up a strand of hair from her shoulder. "I prefer your hair like this, the aftermath of making love with my beautiful wife."

Despite herself, Wren couldn't help the smile that curved her lips. At the same time, her face warmed.

"Take your time. I will be downstairs. Warm water has been brought." Grant kissed her again and then walked out of the room wearing only his shirt and trousers. She was glad to see they dressed casually while at home, as she wasn't sure what to wear.

When she walked to the mirror, she stopped at seeing dried blood on the inside of her thighs. She gasped and ran back to the bed. Pulling back the bedding and seeing a red stain, Wren covered her mouth with both hands. What exactly should she expect to do?

Quickly she went about washing up and dressing, ensuring to be protected in case more blood came. It wasn't time for her courses. Perhaps the excitement had brought blood. Or it could be that marital relations made the woman bleed.

Once she was fully dressed in a blue morning dress with short sleeves and an empire waist, Wren made her way down the stairs and followed the sound of voices to the dining room.

Inside were Grant, Evan, and Felicity. Her sister-in-law stood and came to her, taking her in with her bright eyes. "I was about to come upstairs and see about you. Is everything to your liking?"

"Everything is perfect." Wren managed a smile and then whispered, "I must speak to you about laundering the sheets."

Felicity gave her an understanding look. "No need to worry. They will be changed immediately. The staff will see to it."

"You don't understand," Wren said in an urgent whisper. "They are… I, er…blood," she finally said, sure her face was fire red.

Grant and Even stopped talking and looked at them with curiosity, and Grant's expression turned to worry.

"We will return shortly," Felicity said. "We require a moment to talk about something that is only for women's ears." She threaded her arm through Wrens. "Come. We will go to the sitting room for a bit."

Once they entered the smaller room, Felicity turned to her and gestured to the settee. As they sat, she said, "It is normal for the first time." She then hugged Wren. "I am sure you are shocked. It only happens once. Rest assured."

"I—I wasn't sure. Your staff…"

"Both women, Rosalie and Joan, are married and will not be shocked. If anything, it is a statement that you remained pure until you wed. It's actually a badge of honor, for a bride." She smiled.

Immediately Wren felt better. "So, I will not bleed each time?"

Felicity laughed and took her hands. "You are asking the same questions I did. I raced to my family home and asked Mother all these things."

"Thank you," Wren said, meaning it. If her mother had been alive, she would have done the same, but now, she realized she'd not only gained a husband, but a new sister and she was grateful for it.

When they returned to the dining room, Grant stood and held a chair out for her. He kissed her temple. "Is everything well?"

"Yes," Wren beamed up at him. "Everything is perfect."

Evan nodded in greeting. "We were discussing where you are to live. Grant wishes to rent a townhome. Felicity and I insist you remain here for a few months until you've had time to adjust, and then together you can decide where to live."

Such a decision was impossible. Wren hadn't considered where they'd live. She'd assumed they would remain there since it was where Grant lived. The home was enormous, and it wasn't as if they'd be in each other's way.

"I will leave the decision up to Wren," Grant said and looked at her. "Upstairs on my side of the house, there is my bedchamber, and a water closet, as well as a sitting room and another room that I use as a place to write."

Felicity met her brother's gaze. "It can easily be changed into a sitting room for you and Wren to host company."

"What about my aunt?" Wren asked.

Evan replied, "She can have one of the bedchambers downstairs, or there are two on the second floor. Although the one down here has an adjoining room that she can furnish or decorate as she sees fit. And as she gets older, perhaps she'd appreciate rooms on the lower level so she can easily come and go as she pleases."

They continued to discuss the living situation while Wren busied herself with eating. The food was delicious, and she was ravenous despite having eaten a large dinner the night before.

"I had planned to have a meal brought up to you. It surprised me to see you up and about so early." Felicity winked playfully. "I assumed you'd be exhausted."

"It is later than usual," Grant muttered, giving his sister a narrowed-eye look. "Come, Wren, let us walk about the garden."

It was a bit chilly outside, so Grant placed a shawl over her shoulders. They walked in the garden at a leisurely pace. The air was perfumed by blooms from beautifully blooming gardenias. Wren inhaled deeply, enjoying the flower's gift to those who walked by.

Grant took her shoulders and turned her to face him. "If you wish for us to live elsewhere or remain here, it matters not to me. I want you to be happy and feel comfortable."

"I wish you to be happy and comfortable as well. What were your plans before marrying me? Did you plan to remain here forever?"

When he pulled her against him, she laid her cheek on his chest. Grant's deep voice vibrated in her ear when he spoke. "I planned to remain here for at least another year. Once the ship returned, I hoped to purchase a home. Not a grand one like this one, but more the size of my parents' home. I prefer living closer to town."

He lifted her face. "What about you? In your dreams, what kind of home have you wished for?"

"I wished for a small cottage with a big kitchen, land so I could garden, and a cat to sleep in the sun.

"A cat?" Grant chuckled. "Why a cat and not a dog?"

"Cats are much more independent."

He pressed a soft kiss to her lips. "How about my larger house with a garden and we can then get a cat?"

"I like it." Wren giggled when Grant meowed.

Her husband took her hand, and they continued walking. He looked up to a tree where a bird sang gayly. "I have enough saved to purchase a townhouse. A small one. However, if we wait six months then I will be able to purchase a larger one, which I prefer. Because we will have children, and they will need rooms of their own."

Children! Her heart warmed. "Very well, we remain here until then," Wren answered. They'd made their first important decision together and it felt good. That they were a couple now who would discuss so many other things in the years ahead.

If only her family had lived. They would love Grant. Especially her mother, who'd always insisted Wren marry a handsome man.

"Is something wrong?" Grant stopped and studied her. "If you'd really rather move sooner, just say it and we'll go."

"It's not that," Wren said, cupping his jaw with her palm. "I was considering how much my mum, da, and sister would love you. I was wishing they were here to meet you."

"I am sorry not to have had the privilege of meeting them. You are the walking embodiment of all things good and kind. I imagine it is because you had wonderful parents."

Wren nodded. "They were."

He began walking once more, his hand in Wren's. "We have made our first decision of many. Next, I will give you and Felicity free reign to redecorate the rooms. My statement is only a formality. I am sure my sister already has appointments with decorators."

The relationship between Grant and Felicity was a good one. Wren was glad to see how well they got along. It would make living there much easier.

"Look," Grant pointed to a tree branch where a yellow bird was perched. "A canary!"

"How beautifully it sings," Wren moved closer, and the small bird stopped singing to regard her.

Grant came to stand next to her and whistled at the bird. It cocked its head to the side, its dark eyes intent. "He must have escaped from his cage. Wealthy people like to purchase these rare birds to keep them caged in order to hear their song."

"Will it survive on its own?" Wren asked as the bird resumed its song.

"I am sure the bird is aware of where he lives. For now, he prefers to be free. I will let the staff know to put out breadcrumbs in case it decides to remain."

EVERYTHING WAS DIFFERENT and felt different, Grant mused as he joined his friends at the Grant Hotel. Several gentlemen were there to listen to a lecture from a well-known archeologist who'd recently returned from a dig in Africa.

However, Grant joined Evan, Miles, and Henry in a smaller room that was away from the man's lecture.

"Do we have all the money required?" Evan asked. "Payment must be made by the end of the week."

Everyone turned to Miles, who rolled his eyes. "I had to travel and lost track of time. Therefore, it seems I have lost the bet." His whiskey-colored gaze scanned the room. "I will have the money replenished before the ship returns."

"That is a long time," Evan said, chuckling. "What, six months? We did not have that long."

"The only one that acquired the money and has therefore won is Grant. That means we are each to give him a percentage."

"No," Grant said. "I do not want it. The money came to me in a way that I am not proud of. If anything, I cannot wait for the ship to return so I can repay it."

No one argued, seeming to understand he preferred not to be reminded of the fact he'd earned the money by sleeping with a woman. Especially now that he was married and happily so.

"What if we wager on whether or not Miles will have his money replenished in a month," Henry said.

Evan laughed. "Henry, you are always up for a bet, and I have missed our ridiculous wagers. I wager that Miles will not come up with the money."

"You wound me," Miles replied and sipped from his glass. "What about you?" He looked to Grant.

"What are we wagering?" Grant asked before replying.

They waited for Henry since he'd proposed the wager. With a devilish smile, Henry lifted his glass. "If Miles replenishes his investment in a month, those who doubted him must parade naked at a social event. If he does not, then he, along with the losers, will do so."

"Can it be in the garden?" Evan asked, laughing.

"Within sight," Henry replied.

"I wager Miles will," Grant said, knowing Miles would go to extremes to ensure he won.

"I wager he will not," Henry announced.

They held up their glasses, the wager set.

"Do not begin until after the money is paid to the captain," Henry instructed Miles.

Miles lifted a brow. "Very well."

Grant sat back, not listening to their discussion. Instead, he thought about how he wanted to rush home and see Wren. It was only when he noticed Miles looking at him as if expecting a reply that he stopped musing. "What did you say?"

"I spoke to Mother about hosting a small gathering to celebrate your marriage. It will not do for a friend of mine's wife to be mistreated by the vipers that call themselves 'ladies' in our social circles." Miles' parents, the Duke & Duchess of Spencer, hosting an event for them would ensure Wren's acceptance.

Grant could not believe that Miles would do such a thing. "I don't know what to say. I would be ever so grateful."

Speechless, he met Miles' gaze. The lord nodded, seeming to know he was unable to formulate words. "Mother wishes for it to be in a week."

"Th—that is fine. Miles, you are…"

Lord Johnstone held up his hand to stop him. "Do not say that I am kind or nice. It would ruin my reputation of being cold, heartless, and deplorable."

The other men laughed, as those were the exact words of a woman who had poured her drink on Miles' head several months earlier. They'd been struck silent when it happened, then burst into laughter when Miles blinked, and liquid splashed from his lashes.

Instead of going home after leaving the hotel, Grant went to a small patisserie and purchased a box of delicacies for Wren to try. Then he went to the shop next door and purchased dainty handkerchiefs and gloves. When he exited, a familiar carriage came to a stop in front of the theatre. A familiar man climbed down and assisted a woman.

It was Eleanor Dupree, the woman he'd slept with ten years earlier, and her husband. Theirs was the marriage he'd ruined for many years. As if sensing his regard, the man turned to him and Grant stood still, unable to move. He wanted to go to them and apologize, to explain that he'd not meant to cause such harm. A part of him acknowledged that it was the woman's doing, not just his. But he'd been wrong to go to that house on that wretched evening.

The man nodded in acknowledgment, then turned to smile at the woman who did not notice him, and together they went to the doors. They were together, and Grant was glad. It seemed that after years apart, they'd reconciled. For that, he was grateful.

Once home, he hurried up the stairs and found Wren in the sitting room reading over his book. He froze, and opened his mouth to tell her to stop, but found he didn't have a voice. No one had read his writing, except for perhaps the publishing company he'd mailed a copy to. It was much too personal, and he feared what others would think.

Wren looked up, her face brightening at seeing him. After placing the bound pages down carefully, she hurried to him. "You are a magnificent writer. I am only a few pages in, and the story has gripped me."

"You only say it because I'm your husband," Grant teased, but her words warmed his heart, nonetheless. Even if her opinion was biased, it mattered to him very much and made him proud.

Wren shook her head. "No, if it was rubbish, I would tell you 'good effort', but you must begin writing again." Then the box in his hands took her attention and she studied it. "What is that?"

Grant held them out of her reach. "You can open these, but only if you pay with a kiss."

His heart melted at the flush of her cheeks as she lifted to her toes and shyly pressed a kiss to his lips. How he loved his wife. Everything about her was precious to him.

"I suppose that peck will have to do." He walked to a settee and gestured to it. "Sit, my lady."

Once Wren was seated, he placed the parcels on her lap and joined her.

First, she opened the patisserie box, making soft sounds of appreciation as she looked over the pastries. "How enchanting. I do not wish to ruin them."

"We will eat them anyway." Grant laughed when she held the box away. "Open the other one."

It was the most enjoyable thing to watch as she unwrapped the handkerchiefs and gloves, touching them with reverence.

"These are the most beautiful things I have ever owned," she exclaimed, holding them to her chest.

Such gratitude for such a simple gift, he thought. There would be hard times ahead for them. His social peers would do their best to make Wren aware she was not on their level, and he wished there was something he could do to prevent it. She was unspoiled and so easily pleased, and so different from other women of his stratus.

His opinion was only made more true when she said, "Thank you," and placed the items down carefully before she wrapped her arms around his neck. "You are so wonderful to me."

Grant nuzzled her neck, inhaling the fresh scent of a very light floral. When her breath caught, it was obvious she enjoyed his touches and caresses.

"I want you so much," Grant whispered in her ear, and then traced it with his tongue.

"*Mm mm.*" Wren's fingers slid through his hair.

Already hard as stone, he could not wait to have her again.

They'd made love the night before and again that morning, but as he'd predicted on their wedding night, he was insatiable when it came to Wren.

"Can I?" he asked, trailing kisses from her ear to her jawline and down to the base of her throat, the entire time sliding his hand up her skirt until reaching her thigh. "If you don't want to, just tell me 'no'. I understand."

"I want you too." Wren was breathless, the words barely above a whisper.

After ensuring to move the parcels out of the way, he laid her back onto the settee, pushed her dress up just enough to allow him access, and trailed his tongue up her thigh. Wren trembled.

It was important that Wren was ready for him. He was her first lover and although she was eager, it could be she was still tender. Upon reaching her apex, he slid his tongue between her netherlips slowly, then flicked at the nub with the tip of his tongue.

Wren melted under him as he continued until she reached release, her sex constricting as she let out a long moan.

He was so hard by then that it was almost painful. It took all his willpower not to thrust too fast or deeply. Somehow he managed to enter her, sliding in slowly, allowing for her to stretch to accommodate his girth.

Each movement brought him closer to release. He was so ready and hot for her that it only took several thrusts before searing heat coiled under his shaft. The climax was hard, and he collapsed, shuddering and covering Wren with his body. When he finally was able to move, he lifted himself up to look down at her. "It is hard to control myself with you. I desire you so much, Wren."

"I do not mind. It is quite enjoyable," Wren replied with a saucy smile. "I like that you want me."

"Good, because I do so very much."

Once they repositioned their clothes, he buttoned the front of his trousers and she smoothed her now-crumpled dress, Grant opened the patisserie box and picked an éclair.

When he put the pastry to her mouth, Wren took a bite, chewed, and closed her eyes. "So very delicious." She watched as he too bit off a piece and then took the delicacy from him.

"Now I have some news to share that I think will delight you." Grant kissed a bit of cream from the corner of Wren's mouth and then proceeded to tell her about the gathering that would be held in their honor.

"Miles informed me that his parents, the Duke and Duchess of Spencer, are to hold a social gathering in our honor."

Her eyes rounded. "Oh. That is wonderful. Terrifying, but wonderful." Unexpectedly, Wren began to cry.

He held her tightly, mystified by her reaction. "Why are you crying?"

"Y-your friends are wonderful. Your sister is wonderful. I cannot believe how very fortunate I am to have met you. That they do not shun me is already enough, but that they are to ensure I do not suffer at the hands of unkind people is more than I could ever expect." She sniffled.

"Don't cry. Of course, my friends will do what they can to help. Miles and I are very close, and this is in a way his wedding gift to us. He may seem distant and cold, but believe me, he is one of the kindest people I have had the privilege to know."

"I must speak to Felicity." Wren's disposition changed, and she pushed away from him to stand as she smoothed her skirts and hurried from the room. But first, she bent to give him a kiss. "I'm so happy."

Grant shook his head, glad to have made his new wife so pleased with so little. He lifted the patisserie box and was about to pick a morsel when Wren reappeared and snatched it from his grip.

"If Felicity is to help me prepare for this event, I will pay her with a choice of pastry." With that, she hurried out again.

EPILOGUE

"MILES," HIS MOTHER called out as he walked around the ballroom ensuring everything was in place.

He turned to find his beautiful mother, Her Grace Arabella Johnstone, waving him to come to her.

"Mother, you have outdone yourself." He kissed her cheek, and she waved her hands impatiently.

"Everything has been done, all that we need is to be ready as the first carriages arrive. I wish you to meet someone."

"Mother." He let out a long breath. "I warned you, no matchmaking."

His mother's right eyebrow lifted, a trait they shared when making a point. "Your father and I will have a grandchild before we die. Not just a grandchild, but an *heir*."

"I am the heir," Miles stated, lifting his arm to escort her to the front door. "You and Father could have had another son, who would ensure someone who could carry the title after me."

His mother shook her head. "This delusion of yours not to marry will end. If you do not choose a bride soon, your father and I will."

"I have told you. Once I reach forty, if I am not married, you can arrange a marriage. I do not care to whom. It will be a formality so that I can procreate your much-wanted heir."

"Why are you so unyielding?" His mother gave him an incredulous look. "Did we do something that made you so hard-hearted against marriage?"

He couldn't tell her that the one time he'd fallen in love, it had not only broken his heart but changed how he felt about marriage. He would never allow anyone to have that power over him.

Miles stood dutifully next to his parents to greet the people as the guests arrived. By the time the last people had arrived, he'd lost count of how many eager mothers had thrust their daughters in front of him, espousing the young women's incredible and sometimes unbelievable virtues. If not for standing next to his father, who slid him warning looks every time one of these virtuous misses was presented, he would have burst into laughter several times.

"Come, darling." His mother touched his arm. "I wish you to meet a delightful young woman."

"I've already met all the delightful young women in the room," Miles replied, not moving. "More than enough of them for the night."

She threaded her arm through his. "Come with me."

He allowed it as—never deterred—his mother guided them across the room just as the musicians began the first musical piece of the night.

She stopped in front of one of the overzealous mothers, next to who stood a reasonably attractive younger woman. "Zinnia," his mother began. "I was just telling Miles he should dance with your beautiful Amelia."

Her attention returned to Miles. "Son, this is Amelia Blair."

The young woman, Amelia, stood so straight, he wondered if she could bend. Her nose held up, she scanned him from head to toe as if assessing whether or not he was worthy of a dance.

He had no choice but to appease his mother, at least with one dance. Miles bent at the waist. "Miss Amelia, would you do me the honor of this dance?"

Amelia held out a hand and he took it, placing it into the crook of his arm as he led her to the dance floor where they joined the other dancers.

The entire time he kept an eye on the door for when Grant and Wren arrived. He'd instructed the attendants that they should be announced with much fanfare.

Thankfully, just as the song ended, he noted Grant and his new bride entering. He extricated himself from Amelia. "The guests of honor have arrived."

Somehow, she managed to hold her nose higher. "Oh yes. They are the reason for all of this. I had forgotten."

Her comment reinforced that he would not dance with her again, nor ever seek her company.

Wren Murray was resplendent in a pale green ballgown, long gloves that covered her arms, and an elegant hairstyle. She dressed understatedly without frills or ruffles but somehow was much prettier than most of the women in the room. Once their announcement and introductions were done, his friend neared and shook Miles' hand. "Again, I thank you so much for this."

Miles nodded. "Take her to meet my parents; they are anxious to know what kind of woman can tame a rogue, so they can arm themselves to find a bride for me."

Out of the corner of his eye, he noticed Amelia headed toward him and he pretended not to see her. Hoping to take refuge behind a punchbowl, he hurried to it and rounded the table.

A squeal was followed by cold liquid splashing on his arm and whoever he'd run into. To his horror, a woman was slipping because of his own clumsiness and was about to lose her balance. He took a step toward her, and just as he caught her elbow, his foot slipped on the spilled punch and Miles lost the fight with gravity.

"*Oomph!*" the woman let out a harsh breath as he landed atop her. She went limp and gazed up at him. "Mother will never let me hear the end of this."

Beneath him was the most beautiful creature he'd ever seen. She had an oval face, a pert nose, and hair as dark as midnight. Her pale blue, long-lashed eyes studied him and crinkled into what he could only describe as a playful expression. She took his breath away.

Her pink lips split into a grin, and to his shock, she began laughing while pushing him off.

He managed to stand, then bent and helped her up. Most of the punch had splashed onto her bodice and the floor. Because he'd fallen over her, he remained dry.

"Siobhan, you are making a spectacle of yourself." Amelia had neared and stood with fists at her sides and a furious curl to her upper lip. "You make a mockery of our family with your actions."

His mother rushed over, her gaze moving from the furious Amelia to the still-laughing Siobhan.

"Your grace, I beg you, excuse my sister's actions," Amelia said to his mother then slid another glare at her sister, who gave her a bland look in return. She motioned to Siobhan with one hand. "Apologize to Her Grace."

"It was I who ran into her and caused her to fall," Miles clarified. "It is I who should apologize to you, Miss Blair."

Siobhan shrugged, then noting her mother had neared, straightened, and gave him a soft smile. "No harm has been done, my lord."

"Come, let us try to remedy your ruined dress." Amelia motioned for Siobhan to follow her.

The young beauty slid a glance at him, her eyes moving from his eyes to his lips and then back to meet his gaze. "My lord, I look forward to the rest of this delightful evening."

As the servants quickly cleaned the floor and his mother inspected him to ensure there were no stains, his attention was focused on the young woman being led away from the ballroom.

"No," his mother warned. "The younger Miss Blair is like an untamed cat. She is always causing something dramatic or even scandalous to happen."

"She didn't cause anything. I was the one who ran into her whilst trying to keep away from the eldest," Miles replied. "Besides, Mother, as I previously declared, I have no plan to pursue anyone." He turned to look at his mother, though, he realized, it took an effort. If the younger Miss Blair hadn't just disappeared into the area set apart for the ladies, he supposed, he wouldn't have been able to do so.

His father joined them. "Is everything well?"

"No," his mother replied. "I just saw a gleam in his eye. And it was directed at the worst possible young woman."

At that, Miles shook his head. Perhaps this night would turn out to be much more than another tiresome social gathering. Moments later, he stood before the room with his parents as they congratulated the newlyweds and toasted their happiness.

The gathering would go far into assuring Wren's acceptance into their circles. No one would dare snub her after the display of support by the Duke and Duchess of Spencer. He raised his glass. But then, across the room, movement caught his attention. It was Siobhan, who darted from behind the curtains and through the doors into the garden.

His lips curved. She was a wild one indeed. He drank his champagne and set his glass down on the tray of a passing servant before heading out after her to see what she was going to get up to next.

THE END

About the Author

Most days USA Today Bestseller Hildie McQueen can be found in her overly tight leggings and green hoodie, holding a cup of British black tea while stalking her hunky lawn guy. Author of Medieval Highlander and American Historical romance, she writes something every reader can enjoy.

Hildie's favorite past-times are reader conventions, traveling, shopping and reading.

She resides in beautiful small town Georgia with her super-hero husband Kurt and three little doggies.

Visit her website at www.hildiemcqueen.com
Facebook: HildieMcQueen
Twitter: @HildieMcQueen
Instagram: hildiemcqueenwriter

.

Milton Keynes UK
Ingram Content Group UK Ltd.
UKHW021817010124
435297UK00016B/835